I AM A
TRUCK

MICHELLE WINTERS

I AM A TRUCK

MICHELLE WINTERS

Invisible Publishing
Halifax & Picton

Library and Archives Canada Cataloguing in Publication

Winters, Michelle, 1972-, author
    I am a truck / Michelle Winters.

Issued in print and electronic formats.
ISBN 978-1-926743-78-3 (paperback).--ISBN 978-1-926743-79-0 (epub)

    I. Title.

PS8645.I5762I26 2016   C813'.6   C2016-905502-7
                                               C2016-905503-5

Edited by Leigh Nash

Cover and interior design by Megan Fildes | Typeset in Laurentian
With thanks to type designer Rod McDonald

Printed and bound in Canada

Invisible Publishing | Halifax & Picton
www.invisiblepublishing.com

We acknowledge the support of the Canada Council for the Arts which last year invested $20.1 million in writing and publishing throughout Canada.

 Canada Council   Conseil des Arts
for the Arts   du Canada

When you don't feel it it shows they tear out your soul
And when you believe they call it rock and roll

— Spoon, "The Beast and Dragon, Adored"

For Nipper and Heidi

NOW

The Silverado was reported sitting next to the highway with the driver-side door open just eight hours after Agathe had kissed Réjean on the front step of their cottage and sent him off fishing in the rain with a Thermos full of coffee, four sandwiches au bologne, and a dozen date squares. It was pouring so hard that as they embraced, the rain smacked loudly on Réjean's enormous back. He blew her a kiss as he reversed out of sight, and she smiled and touched her lips.

He was lying to her. She had known from the second he came home the night before and experimentally said, "Hé, sais-tu quoi?" As he told her the lie, she studied him, half-amused, waiting for him to crack. He was an awful liar, but he persevered artlessly in his tale of a fishing trip on Saturday with the men from work. Their twentieth wedding anniversary was next week and Agathe wasn't about to challenge him on trying to cover up a surprise for her. In fact, she was relieved. Réjean had been so odd lately—distracted, distant...Only in bed was he fully engaged, and there they were trying something new. Their physical relationship had flourished over the years, despite the normalcy and tedium innate in all couples, and despite what Agathe considered to be the loss of her figure. As early as her twenties, her body had succumbed to a condition that afflicted generations of women in her family: a ballooning of her upper half, while her legs remained coltish and slim. As her top half grew, the weight strained her spine, giving her a subtle hunch that would grow more pronounced as the years wore on. But every new pound only enticed Réjean more as he kissed and bit and squeezed her extra flesh. For him, she would always be the girl who had awakened his soul that July day at the marché when they were teenagers.

Agathe had been watching the eaves for birds while her mother examined potatoes. When Réjean suddenly appeared, his eyes already on her, he saturated her field of vision. Agathe's knees buckled and she slid to the ground. Édithe Thibeault was quick and sharp, tossing the bag of potatoes into the air and catching her daughter before she hit the ground. As the potatoes rained down, Édithe looked up and also set disbelieving eyes on Réjean. At only fifteen, he was close to seven feet tall, with a chest as big as a rain barrel and arms the size of a normal man's legs. His hands were like a bunch of bananas. He was already working on the downy beginnings of his moustache. For her part, Agathe had just the year before peeled her way out of a rind of unremarkability, emerging that summer a very pretty girl. Her mother's friends would comment that Agathe was now pretty enough to be a newscaster or a figure skater and that perhaps, her beauty would be the thing to finally put P'tit Village on the map. For Réjean, she became existence itself. He broke from his brothers and swept in, hands extended, and, without a word, pulled up both Agathe and her mother so that their feet briefly left the ground. His eyes locked on to Agathe's until he turned to join his brothers, gazing over his shoulder at her. When she had finally lost sight of his back in the crowd, Agathe began to cry.

On returning from the market, Réjean asked his mother for a haircut and presented himself at the Thibeaults' door later that same afternoon, hair clippings still in his ears, asking if Agathe would like to go for a walk. He couldn't have expected that once they reached the woods at the end of the street, Agathe would grab him and pull him to her, knocking the breath out of them both. They had to wait three years to get married.

They'd learned early on that Agathe was missing one of the parts needed to make babies, which made them sad at first, then overjoyed when they realized they didn't want babies, only each other. "Il n'y a que nous," they would say, making a tunnel between their eyes with their hands.

Réjean said that the fishing trip should be wrapped up by dinnertime. Even if the fishing part wasn't true, he wasn't so foolish as to lie about when he would be home. Agathe had nearly eight hours to work on her surprise for him.

From between the box spring and mattress, she pulled her bloc-notes and pencils. They had agreed this year they would make gifts for each other. She had been toiling solidly for two weeks while Réjean was at work. She brought her materials to the table, put on a pot of tea, and emptied the ashtray. Agathe had initially started smoking as a means of trying to control her weight, but her top half only continued to swell—along with a new love of cigarettes.

She flipped to her drawing on the pad. It wouldn't matter that she was working from a photo in the newspaper; it looked enough like the Silverado that Réjean wouldn't know the difference. Agathe was pleased with just how much her drawing resembled the photo, and planned to put the picture in a frame she had taken from a watercolour painting in the basement.

Réjean had never owned anything but a Chevy and revered the brand with a feverish loyalty. Every year, he replaced his current truck with the newest model, not because the old one was lacking or showing signs of wear, but because every truck that Chevy brought out Réjean would declare more phenomenal than the last. He often lost himself in grateful praise of the corporation for designing such a sturdy vehicle with such excellent handling.

"C'est un beau truck, ça."

Not long after they were married, the lumber work in P'tit Village began to dwindle, but Réjean had heard that it was plentiful in nearby English-speaking Pinto. They moved into a cottage in the woods there, and began a life of increasing seclusion, and the prospect of communicating only with each other in a town where no one spoke French. Agathe and Réjean understood English, but held it in heavy contempt—even if English made up half the French they spoke. At home and school, they had been taught that the Anglophone world was trying to oppress them, monopolize their culture, and eradicate their language. It was safest to agree. Being separated by language from the world around them strengthened their bond of exclusivity. Gradually, they retreated from the world altogether, existing solely for each other in the confines of their home.

"Il n'y a que nous."

The hours sped by as Agathe worked, capturing every realistic inch, the darks and lights, blending bits of pencil with the twisted end of a tissue and her fingers. Smudging the lines was her favourite part. It looked so real. In real life, things were smudgy. As she reproduced the positive and negative spaces of the photo, she imagined what she and Réjean might try out when he returned that night. Perhaps they could include the Silverado. She thought about a game where she was a truck driver and Réjean a trusting hitchhiker, until the sun went orange in the sky and she remembered dinner.

If Réjean was any kind of liar, he would bring home fish, even if it meant buying it at the store. She would need to assist the lie by anticipating fish and making something complementary. She would make scalloped potatoes. Scalloped potatoes were always appropriate.

She hid her drawing back beneath the mattress and returned to the kitchen, where she devoted herself to the extra-thin slicing of potatoes and onions, loading the first layer into the pan, nearly skipping to the refrigerator for more cheese.

When she heard Réjean pull into his spot in front of the house, she checked the kitchen for any pencil-darkened clues. But as her eyes passed the window and stopped on the spot where the Silverado should be, she found it occupied by a police cruiser. There were two officers up front, who talked for a moment in the car before making their way to the door and knocking gently.

"Good evening, ma'am. Are you the wife of Réjean Lapointe?"

"Ouah..."

"Does your husband drive a black Chevrolet Silverado?"

"Ouah..."

"Would it be all right if we came in?"

They stood inside the door, because she didn't invite them to sit, and asked a lot of rude questions about Réjean and their relationship: Did he seem happy? Were they having any problems in their marriage?

"Beunh, non," she replied emphatically, and told them

about their upcoming anniversary and the surprise he was without question preparing right now.

"Has he been distracted or at all different lately? Anything unusual?"

Agathe reached for her cigarettes.

"Ma'am, your husband's empty truck was reported not far from here, sitting on the shoulder with the driver-side door open. Do you have any idea why that might be?"

She did not.

"The good news is it doesn't look like there's been any foul play or an accident. It's more like he just…walked away. We're still trying to get a feel for the situation, ma'am. Most times these cases turn out to have a perfectly reasonable explanation. Sometimes people have a strange way of sending a message—"

"Sending un message," Agathe cut him off. "Comme quoi, un message? Pour qui? Pour moi?"

The other officer stepped in. "We just want to make sure we have all the details before we start speculating on what might have happened, ma'am."

They told her to call if she had any information that might lead to finding him and promised she would be the first to know if they heard anything. As she closed the door behind them, she leaned her shoulder against it and studied the floor. Her mind had been so consumed with dislike for the policemen that she hadn't considered how strange it was, Réjean's truck at the side of the road, without Réjean. But now that the officers were climbing back into the cruiser, she was struck by the absolute impossibility of him leaving the truck of his own volition. This didn't feel like part of a surprise; this felt like something going wrong. Her insides tightened. Réjean abandoning the Silverado?

No. She couldn't imagine him just walking away. Then, as she tried to picture it, her heart suddenly went cold.

The army man.

Réjean had seen Agathe and the army man together, she knew it. She now felt sure he knew she'd lied about it. She couldn't tell, as they'd driven home in silence, whether she'd convinced him. But Réjean had been intensely preoccupied. Had he been plotting the whole way home how he would punish her? Was he trying to scare her? Or did he feel so betrayed by her indiscretion that he was willing to sacrifice the Silverado to be rid of her? No, Réjean wouldn't do that. Or would he? She'd been trying to ignore his recent strangeness, even before the army man, but wished now that she had said something. She'd had so many chances. They both knew things felt different. But last night while they played gin rummy and she baked date squares, the few times Réjean was present enough to look directly at her, there was a distress in his eyes that had nothing to do with their anniversary. It had to do with the army man. She tried to picture what Réjean had seen, and how awful it must have looked from his perspective. She needed to let him know that it wasn't what he thought.

The police officer's words ran through her mind: *It's more like he just...walked away.*

If Réjean was alive, she would find him. She ran to the bedroom and retrieved her bloc-notes, flipping her Silverado drawing over the coils of the pad. She would put up posters all over town. Someone had to know where he was. She concentrated on the empty page and pulled the cap off a black marker, thinking about the word for a moment before covering a third of the page in big block letters that spelled *MISSING*.

THEN

Réjean and Agathe were in the Silverado for a drive. Réjean had put on a clean flannel shirt, slapped a giant handful of musky aftershave on either side of his face, and groomed his moustache. Agathe admired him from the passenger seat as they travelled the wooded roads they felt they owned.

Réjean played the French folk-music station with the sound turned down to a whisper. He enjoyed music exactly as much as he did the hum of the engine and tried to create a balance between the two. While Agathe loved to see him so content, the music and its volume had set her teeth on edge since the first time they'd climbed into a vehicle together. It was so...fragile. Agathe longed for a crescendo, some histrionics, something loud to release the strap of tension in her jaw. She turned toward the window and opened her eyes wide, trying to take an interest in the landscape. She bumped her head rhythmically against the window frame, staring into the endless ranks of trees whipping past. What writhing mass of wildness went on in there when no one could see? Fanged, incandescent reptiles, prehistoric bugs, rainbow-swirly birds...

"Viens voir l'Acadie" was playing. It played every day; the French folk-music canon had hard limits. The sound had gone from a nagging drone to a roar, and bumping her head against the window frame was not scratching the itch.

There had been no rock and roll for Agathe growing up. It was not a welcome form of entertainment in P'tit Village.

She remembered her father reading the newspaper after dinner one night, and letting out a loud "Tsk." He shook his head and held out the page to a picture of a dark-haired woman with short hair and raccoon eyes, wearing a ripped black T-shirt and leather pants, playing guitar on a stage. "Le rockandroll," he'd muttered. Later that night, Agathe had dug the paper out of the garbage, and with her hands covered in chicken grease and coffee grounds, a feeling awoke in her like her head was rising into the clouds. It was hard to say whether the ascent was one of flying or of actually growing taller—but either way, it felt like something she needed. But, as her family and Réjean and her entire town embraced one style of music and reviled rock and roll's Anglophone roots, her life developed without it. Although she would sometimes hear it nearby, it was never close enough to take hold.

Réjean began to tap his wedding ring against the wheel to a non-existent rhythm, and without meaning to, Agathe turned suddenly from the window and said, "Réjean, y-a-t'il pas d'autre musique?"

"Autre musique," he said, looking down at the radio, "ben, comme quoi, autre musique?"

"'Ché pas!" She took a breath. "Les kids, là, ça écoute le rockandroll. C'est populaire, ça."

"Le rockandroll," said Réjean, incredulous.

"Ouah!" said Agathe, reaching for the dial. As she fiddled through static and talk, Réjean gripped the wheel and set his eyes dead ahead.

At least two, but maybe eight, guitars all started playing at the same time, driving—piledriving—through the speakers, and Agathe felt the hinges in her jaw loosen. Réjean burst out laughing. "Ça?" he snorted. From the radio, the guy with all the guitars asked the lord to take him downtown so he could find himself some tush.

"Écoute comme c'est excitant, Réjean. Ça bouge!" she said, holding both hands out to the radio, as if to feed him handfuls of it.

"O, Agathe," he laughed. "Ah non. Ah non. Non. Tellement stupide cette musique...Écoute ça," he said disgustedly.

"C'est nouveau," she said. "T'as pas envie de quelque chose de nouveau?"

"C'est pas même français!" he cried.

She knew how he was going to be, and it wasn't worth it.

"Crisse que t'es bébé, sometimes. Franchement..."

She switched the dial through the static back to the churchy singsong of the French folk station. "Voilà ta musique, bébé."

Réjean reached for her hand and kissed it. "Merci, mon trésor," he said, triumphantly. "Notre musique, ça."

She turned toward the window and fell asleep.

Rock and roll filled the truck as Agathe drifted out of a shallow nap. She smiled as she reached out for Réjean, thinking he had changed his mind and put the music on for her, but she touched only his empty seat. The smell of toasted buns let her know that they were at the Lobster Shack. Réjean must have felt bad about the radio squabble and was buying her a lobster roll. There was a roadside stand for lobster rolls every kilometer or so in Pinto, but Lobster Shack was her favorite. She kept her eyes closed and concentrated on the music she now realized was coming from the vehicle parked next to them. The loud, ominous song shuddered in, lifting her skin from her bones. She opened her eyes just enough to see the driver turn off the engine, holding the key in the ignition so the radio could go on playing. From where her head rested against the passenger-side window, she looked directly at him, separated by their two window frames. He was a big man, dressed in army attire, singing along. He caught sight of Agathe's face propped against the frame. She grinned drowsily. The man turned in his seat and focused intently on her. He continued singing—to her—nodding more vigorously. When the song had built to a peak, he pointed for her to sing with him, sing for the years, sing for the laughter, sing for the tears.

She laughed despite herself, and her palms started to sweat. The drums announced something momentous, and the man held up a fist and sang for her to dream on until her dreams came true. Agathe laughed helplessly. She glanced at the driver-side mirror and saw Réjean at the counter of the Lobster Shack up the hill.

The man sang still higher, and as he did, he spread his fingers and let the song flood through, as though he had been holding it in his clenched fist, his voice disintegrating into an animal shriek—aAaAaAaAaAaAaAaAaA!

It was then she saw the dust kicking up behind Réjean in the rear-view mirror.

"Aie, va-t-en!" she hissed, waving the man away with both hands.

The man spread his palms in the same theatrical way he had with the pointing and made a mock hurt face.

"Allez-y," she rasped more loudly. "Il va te tuer."

The man reacted to the change on her face and turned to see what caused it.

"*Go!*" she shouted.

At the sight of Réjean's thunderous approach, the man

threw the truck into gear, playfully shaking a scolding finger at Agathe. He peeled out of the lot, pointed meaningfully back at her, and raised his fist in the air.

Réjean slapped both hands against the door frame. "Agathe! Qu'est-ce qu'il t'a dit?"

"O, Réjean," she said, "c'était un psycho. J'étais tellement scared, mais y est parti, y est parti."

Réjean reached through the window and gathered her up in his arms, and Agathe tried not to smile as she watched the man disappear down the road.

NOW

Réjean was filed as a Voluntary Missing Adult, and the police again promised to let Agathe know the moment they heard anything. Considering his size, there was an assumption he'd left of his own free will. It didn't look as though he'd been kidnapped or harmed. The police seemed convinced he'd come back if he wanted to.

Agathe awoke the day of their anniversary to the sound of gravel crunching out front and ran to the window to see a tow truck dragging the Silverado. Her confused heart started to pound. She looked hard, searching for him in the hitched-up truck, and held her breath as she opened the door to a guy in green coveralls who gave her a sheepish look as he held up the keys and asked if she wanted him to drive it into the garage for her.

She stood in the garage and smoked, looking at the truck.

The Silverado was a living metaphor for Réjean, a physical manifestation of the man who wasn't coming home. *Why wasn't he coming home?*

She pitched her cigarette and fell toward the truck, throwing her arms around the driver side.

"Où es-tu, Réjean?" she keened, her face smudging the liquid black finish. "Où es-tu?"

She slid her hands down and kissed the window. She brought her forehead to rest on the frame, squeezed her eyes shut tight, and lifted the door handle.

The smell of his aftershave hit her in an agonizing wave,

and she threw herself face first on the seat, grasping at the upholstery, the wheel, the head rest...All these things had held Réjean.

Réjean.

Another wave hit her and she abandoned all restraint and released the first long, loud sob with her face in the flocked velour. What was he doing? What was he doing *out there*? She coughed out three uncontrollable, athletic sobs. The tears kept coming, soaking the seat covers. She bellowed mightily, forcing the sadness out, and was starting to feel crazed from the enterprise. Her muscles and lungs spasmed from fatigue, and she heaved a last sob, panting, unfulfilled, and let her head drop so that her eyes came square with a brown paper bag under the passenger seat.

Son lunch.

She dove for the bag, scraping her arm against the seat recline track, choking back another torrent of tears when her hand grazed the downy carpet of the pants protector—Réjean kept them so clean. She righted herself and clutched the bag to her chest, reliving the feeling of anticipation as she had prepared his sandwiches that morning, the giddy excitement of a surprise. The feeling of knowing he would come home.

She gently uncrumpled the bag and peeked in at the cloud of torn waxed paper that she had smoothed, folded, and tucked seven days ago. This was the closest she'd been to Réjean in a week, and she steadied herself as she prepared to touch perhaps the last thing he had touched. She reached in a trembling hand, pulled out a fluff of paper, and peeled back a corner to reveal the stiffened edge of a sandwich au bologne and the two beneath it. She had packed four. Agathe blacked out all her thoughts but the missing sandwich, and it materialized in her mind, with her inside of it, between two slices of baloney. She imagined herself covered in butter and mustard, being chewed up by Réjean's powerful molars.

Setting the waxed-paper package down beside her, she thrust her hand back in the bag. The date squares. Agathe's date squares were so popular with Réjean's co-workers that she had made sure to send him off fishing with a solid dozen. There were nine petrified ones left, lying in disarray in a tuft of mangled paper.

Agathe called the police and asked that they come to the house right away. When they arrived, she dropped the lunch bag on the kitchen table and folded her arms.

"Et?" she said.

The officers said nothing.

"C'est ben son lunch. Y'avait laissé dans le truck."

"Right," said the older officer.

"Ben, ça veut dire quoi, ça? N'est-ce pas de l'évidence? To find him?"

"I'm sorry, ma'am. It doesn't really tell us anything."

She grabbed the bag and pulled it open. "Garde! Yate some!"

"All right," said the officer.

Agathe laid her palms flat on the table and leaned across it. "What. Does. It. Meen?

"I'm sorry, ma'am, there's not much we can do with it."

"Alors, je le garde?"

"I suppose so, ma'am."

"Je garde son lunch."

"It's not being held in evidence, ma'am."

She lit a cigarette and looked at them, exhaling slowly. "Vous savez toujours rien."

"We…just haven't received any information."

"Voyons, yé big comme crisse. How you can lose him?"

"Honestly, ma'am, we're doing everything we can. He seems to have just vanished. Are you sure he wasn't in any trouble? Didn't have any enemies?"

"Ben là, y didn't même have any friends. Ce n'était que moi."

After the officers left, Agathe climbed into bed without undressing, pulled her knees up, and crouched under the bedclothes. She felt as though her flesh had been replaced with that of another animal. A fat, solid animal with a rigid hide. A boar, or a rhino. She gazed into the darkness and asked, "Est-ce ma faute?"

She was starting to feel more and more that she knew the answer. Every time an image of the Lobster Shack parking lot, or the face of the army man, or the sound of rock and roll, slipped into her mind, she would chase it away. And every time an image of Réjean's face drifted into her thoughts, she would force her eyes open, though they would seize and sting with tears, and she would resist, making a pinched mask of her features. This would begin to sculpt the topography of her face, defining and eroding her daily, digging a deep crevasse between her brows and gradually pushing her eyes ever so slightly from their sockets.

The days without Réjean were endless. At first, Agathe would wake up in the morning, call the police station ("Toujours rien?"), then ride the bus for the day, putting up posters with his picture and their phone number, asking strangers if they had seen him, searching for any sign. He was *somewhere*; the physical entity of him was just, for now, not here.

Réjean was still alive. The police had said there was no

sign of a struggle, no body recovered—all of which she held
to be excellent signs of his possible return. But what she had
to invariably consider, too, was that the policemen might be
right—that wherever he was, he was there willingly. It was
physically impossible to make Réjean do something against
his will. He was alive and he had opened his lunch and
hadn't bothered to rewrap it for later, because he knew he
wouldn't need it. Then he had tossed the bag carelessly on
the floor and left it. She could picture it now. It didn't make
sense before, the ease of his disappearance. But now, when
she thought of his recent strange behaviour, it made more
sense. She could imagine him walking away now, leaving
the Silverado as easily as he'd left behind his lunch, cutting
all ties from his life with her. A sting like poison squiggled
through her veins, more powerful than any dark feeling
she had allowed herself since the Silverado was discovered.
Under the covers, she squeezed her arms around her bent
knees. She thought of Réjean's abandoned sandwiches,
once soft and edible, now fossilized, and understood she
would have to start looking for a job.

THEN

Réjean Lapointe sat in the scratchy grey swivel chair, *his* chair, across the desk from Martin Bureau. He absently swirled his glass of rum, looking admiringly out the window of the portable trailer at the brand-new Silverado, which was about to become the eighth truck he would buy from Martin at the Chevy dealership.

Martin was filling out the paperwork in his swirly handwriting, occasionally stealing quick glances at Réjean, looking for signs of boredom or impatience. He marvelled at the big man's stillness, at his comfort sitting in a room with another man in silence. Martin recoiled from silence almost as much as he did from conversation. While he recognized the need for verbal communication in his job, and despite the fact that sales talk hinged mainly around a handful of regurgitated jokes, such intercourse terrified him.

More frightening than sales talk for Martin Bureau was small talk. He knew that it was polite to make it, that every sale required some, and that it was essential to humans' ability to coexist, but Martin always feared he might just run out of things to say midway. He never knew how long he would be able to keep going before he shut down, and sometimes felt so bored by what he was saying to another person that he wondered whether he should shut his mouth and let them both off the hook. But that would leave them in laborious silence and he didn't know which was worse.

Early on he had developed a sensitivity to signs of an

interlocutor's desire to bring the conversation to an end and he spent much of his time trying to determine whether or not this was happening. His neurosis made car sales a poor career choice, but he had stumbled into it because he hadn't gone to university, possessed few skills, and had no experience doing anything else.

He was also physiologically predisposed against a life in sales. Martin was what the doctor referred to as a "sweater." He sweated unconcealably and uncontrollably. He sweated sitting perfectly still at his desk and could soak an entire jacket over the course of a sale. It was a cold, nervous sweat, a clamminess felt by every client whose hand he clasped. He was not suited for a career of hand-shaking. He would search the other person's face for signs of disgust and was always impressed by their ability to conceal it, though he would sometimes catch them wiping a palm down their pant leg afterwards.

Martin was not overweight, or not very overweight, and so could not attribute his dampness to excess pounds or poor health. Martin was soft, he was flaccid, but not *fat*. Not officially. His body was simply composed of a little bit of muscle blanketed in a generous covering of doughy white flesh. He daydreamed about how much easier life would be had he grown into a good-looking, muscular, dry-palmed man. But he would never be muscular, no matter how hard he might try, because he didn't like physical activity. It made him sweat.

In spite of his ineptitude with the public, Martin had the highest sales numbers at the dealership. No one who spent even a few moments with Martin Bureau would ever say he was capable of deceiving them. He told the truth no matter how uncomfortable a situation it created. In his stalwart commitment to soldier through a verbal exchange to its conclusion, he would say just about anything. As a result, he revealed intimate details about his own loneliness and personal habits. He instilled in the clientele a sense of control, which gave them confidence, but also the feeling they were helping out a guy who could really use the sale. People bought a lot of cars from Martin Bureau.

As he looked up again from the paperwork at Réjean, Martin got the feeling that he was not so much staring out the window at his truck now as simply staring. Réjean still swirled his glass of rum, not noticing the sloshes that escaped over the rim. Martin had never seen him so distracted.

The day, years ago, that Réjean Lapointe strode across the lot, filling his nostrils with the licorice scent of the new models, the camaraderie between Réjean and Martin was established immediately. Réjean loved Chevy trucks and Martin happened to sell them.

Réjean had approached Martin, wearing beneath his formidable moustache the smile of a child at the gates of an amusement park. When he noticed Martin's name tag, Réjean gave his head a shake and held aloft a great paw.

"Aie, un francophone! C'va bien aller. Y sont beau les new Chevy, hein?" he enthused, pumping Martin's small hand inside his own.

Despite having a French first and last name, Martin spoke no French and usually joked about the fact as an opener in his self-deprecating sales routine. He would say, "Me j'excuse, nein sprechen sie deutsch." It made him cringe to say, but it had the dual effect of reassuring the customer that not only was he not French, but also that he found the French ridiculous. The customer would laugh in agreement that other languages were indeed funny, and so it was established that they were on the same team.

He looked up into Réjean's handsome face for a moment, filled with regret at knowing not a single word of the language that his name misled others to believe he spoke. He winced only a little, as if expecting a blow.

"Oh God, I feel really awkward," he said.

Needing to redeem himself, and not yet ready to give up on a potential sale, Martin asked, his hand still ensconced, if Réjean would like to hear a joke. He'd thought this one up the other night, and hadn't yet tried it out on the other sales guys, whose ongoing pastime it was to mock rival automakers using the letters making up their names.

Réjean cocked his head.

"What does FORD stand for?"

Réjean shrugged.

"Fast. Only. Running. Downhill," said Martin, pausing after each word.

Réjean stared at him for a moment as he processed the information, then resumed shaking Martin's hand with even greater vigour, seemingly indifferent to its dampness, chuckling silently as his dark eyes crinkled. Martin had made a joke about a Ford.

The value of humour among men was just one of the lessons Martin had learned from his father, Jack Bureau—humour, and Lamb's Navy Rum.

Trying to make enough paper noise, Martin pushed the ownership documentation toward Réjean, whose attention could not be drawn away from the lot outside. He held the pen in midair for a few silent moments, then lifted it into Réjean's field of vision.

"Réjean," Martin tried to whisper, so as not to disturb him, while disturbing him.

"Ah, oui," Réjean said, his mind returning. "Oui."

"Is there something you'd like to talk about?" asked Martin, hopefully.

Réjean looked into his rum, then up at Martin. "Non," he said. "C'est un beau truck."

Martin decided to start learning French the day he met Réjean. He sent away for instructional books and cassettes to listen to as he slept, repeated phrases after the mechanical recorded voice on the tape, conjugated verbs in his head and sought out any bilingual signage that could be found on the lot at work.

Les objets dans le miroir sont plus près qu'ils ne paraissent.

His family's French ancestry had been a source of difficulty for Martin growing up, and he solidly resisted learning the language. French was mandatory on the curriculum at school and widely hated by the students, who refused to retain a single lesson. Their irritation at having to study it was transferred to Martin. French was stupid, Martin was French, and his last name in French meant *desk*, which was a stupid name. But when Réjean Lapointe opened his mouth that day in the Chevy lot, Martin had never heard anything more red-blooded. He hadn't known that the language could sound so authoritative. So masculine. In his head, he played out the scene of their first meeting at the dealership—only in his dream version, he was fluently bilingual. He envisioned the jovial exchange they would have, to the exclusion of everyone around them.

He was cautious not to let on to the other guys at the dealership that he was learning French, which made it extra-strange when they saw him talking to himself on the lot. Martin found that the more emphasis you lent the statement, the easier it was to say. He didn't realize how clearly he was shaping words with his lips, especially when he was trying to mentally assume an expression particular to Réjean, a long, low sound, a *beunh*, accompanied most times by an actual shrug, or a tone that implied a shrug. The shrug and noise together communicated that the idea being conveyed was abundantly obvious, but was also like saying "well," or "come on." It was wonderfully French. *Beunh*.

Martin carried on simple exchanges in his head, mutely emoting as he asked himself what he felt like for dinner while maintaining an internal monologue on his activities in the kitchen as he prepared it. Je prépare du spaghetti. He would list everything he drove past on his way to work: une maison, des arbres, de la neige, de la neige, de la neige, encore des arbres...Voici un client, he mused when the door of the dealership swung open at the hand of a customer.

The idea of getting caught talking to himself was not nearly so concerning as getting caught talking to himself in French, not only because of his feared perception of the language, but also because it reeked of a childish attempt to impress Réjean Lapointe. The sales guys all knew Réjean. He was impossible to ignore. They had all watched that first day as he walked across the lot, when by some miracle Martin Bureau had made him laugh. After that, the guys knew Réjean belonged to Martin.

Though his delivery was unpolished, Martin was surprised to find that he sounded informed and confident when speaking French. Like a film detective. But what became increasingly clear, as his French improved, was that the longer he kept it to himself, the less likely it would be that he would be able to use it to converse with Réjean; he couldn't just start speaking French years later. He worried he would never be able to share his love of the language and would have to carry the secret around, undivulged, just like the *other* thing he needed to keep Réjean from finding out.

During Réjean and Martin's very first test drive together—a boxy but agile Chevy Fleetside—Réjean tuned the radio to the French folk station at a barely audible volume, and he and Martin headed out of town. As a rural driver, Réjean needed a test drive on rugged terrain to know whether a vehicle suited his needs. They didn't speak or look at each other much, except when Réjean was impressed by a feat of sensitive handling or braking, and he would share a nod of appreciation with Martin, who spent nearly the entire time looking out the window, really enjoying the ride. His role as salesman was eclipsed by Réjean's knowledge of the product. Réjean didn't need any pitch, just the keys. As such, Martin could enjoy the plush interior and the smoothness of the suspension without having to think of things to say about them. He was, for once, completely comfortable in silence. It was this overwhelming ease that compelled him to suddenly declare, "This is nice."

Before Martin had a chance to regret having ruined the moment, Réjean nodded and smiled.

As they got to know each other over the course of yearly visits at first, when Réjean traded in the previous year's truck for the newest model, then increasingly frequent ones, Réjean came to appreciate Martin's expertise in the purchase of trucks. But it was during that first test drive that Martin's candour—his fearlessness in announcing the niceness of a moment to a complete stranger—made Réjean feel he could tell him anything. He'd never met a man so open. Réjean was also aware of Martin's fear of and admiration for him, which made him even easier to like. The reverence shown to him by other men was never lost on Réjean, but Martin's inability to conceal his awe compelled Réjean to gently push the limits, just to see what a little provocation could produce in someone so sincere. He had also gotten to know the finer points of Martin's fussiness and found them funny.

On his desk, Martin had a holder for his pens that acted as a partition between himself and the person across from him. The holder contained a solid row of identical black pens, all with the clip facing left. There were other writing implements and accessories on his desk in an adjacent trough, but only the pens went in the holder. One day, when Réjean had dropped by to praise the handling of his new S-10 in a hairpin turn, he reached out and, without breaking eye contact with Martin, extracted a pen from the holder. He dawdled with it, describing the vehicle's traction in rounding the sharp bend near the ferry landing, before placing the pen back in the holder, turning it deliberately until the clip was facing right. He sat back and shrugged.

Martin gazed back over his pen holder at Réjean, exhilarated by the provocation. He watched the amusement in Réjean's eyes as he twisted the cap of the pen so the clip was uniformly facing left with the rest, remarking how this year Chevy had brought in a machine from Germany that tested the handling of each vehicle over one hundred and fifty times on a razor-sharp turn. Then he sat back in his chair, daring him to do it again.

That night, Martin went out and bought a bottle of Lamb's Navy Rum in preparation for Réjean's next visit. Thereafter, Réjean would show up unannounced, usually toward the end of the day, and they would face each other across Martin's metal desk and have a drink—sometimes talking, sometimes not. It was nice.

NOW

Réjean had been gone for eighteen days when Agathe was hired at Stereoblast, the store selling gently used electronics in Convenience Place Mall. She tried to keep her mind off Réjean while she was at work, and had never mentioned to Tony and Wood at Stereoblast that she was married. But on the calendar at home, she counted off every day he didn't return. He was alive, she was sure of it, somewhere else, while she was missing him—missing him under the covers of the bed, missing him huddled amid his shirts on the closet floor, missing him curled up in the driver seat of the Silverado. She sat at his chair at the kitchen table and slept on his side of the bed. Taking up his space made him a little less gone. She was walking around in his body and when she caught glimpses of herself in the mirror, Réjean's reflection would look back. With no information whatsoever about his whereabouts, it was hard to know whether to start moving on or continue loving him in his absence. Now when she watched the door at night, she was less and less convinced he would walk through it. The belief was dying on its own, but she felt compelled to keep it alive. Because it was a kind of perverse torture, she would sneak off on her breaks from Stereoblast to visit the Big and Tall section at Hickey's Family Apparel, where she'd bought Réjean three new shirts, every year, for twenty Christmases.

As she approached the main entrance to the mall, the crazy guy in the yellow raincoat was already holding the door open for her. She'd watched him and knew that he held out his hand for change from everyone else but her. She wondered whether it was because she looked like she didn't have any.

Inside Hickey's, she planted her gaze on the far wall where the sign said *Men's*, undertaking the tremulous journey across the beige carpet embossed with chocolate-brown Hs. She passed the two beauty consultants in Cosmetics who at first would leap from their perches to spritz her with perfume and now only followed her lazily with their eyes. She huffed through the hosiery department, where the curvy silhouettes of calves and ankles sprouted from the tops of racks like sexy blades of grass, through the reds and blues of the Children's section with its teeming barrel of Lego, before penetrating the Big and Tall section, located between two racks of ties. The shelves were arranged in a three-quarter circle, obscuring her from most sides so she didn't have to pretend she was shopping.

The shirts were tidy today, the packages correctly sorted by size. Sometimes people would put them back in the wrong place, and you'd have to dig through to find the XXXL ones. Finding one felt like winning a prize. Today the XXXLs were all together at the end, a red-and-green check at the top of the stack. She would probably have bought Réjean this very shirt. Despite their triple-weave durability, a few months of vigorous wear in the woods would leave his work shirts pilled and thinning at the elbows. Réjean wore the life out of his shirts.

She sneaked her index finger through the seam in the plastic packaging, crinkling it as little as possible, until her hand could fit inside, and laid it flat over the spot where his heart would go. Her fingers lingered over to the top button of the cardboard-reinforced collar and the feeling of abandon spread out from her abdomen. She exhaled to steady herself as she unbuttoned it, careful not to make herself known. Her face slackened as she slipped completely into the illusion of Réjean's throat, his collarbone…The softness of the flannel brought back the smell of pine chips, sweat, and aftershave that used to make her drop to her knees in the laundry room and bury her face in the mountain of plaid heaped in the basket before she surrendered it to the washing machine. So much of Réjean was left behind in his work shirts—his warmth, his breath, his flesh and bones and blood, the very *himness* of him. Washing his shirts used to feel like washing a little bit of him away, and left her with a mild sadness that required she smoke a cigarette.

Thinking about his sternum as she unbuttoned the next button, she unexpectedly moaned. She froze, clutching the shirt as though the two of them had been caught together. Just beyond the rack, a man primly cleared his throat.

Snatching her hand from the package, she sped from the shirt racks, nearly bowling over the nosy menswear clerk who remembered her from the days when she used to buy things.

She rummaged for her cigarettes, put one in her mouth, and had it lit before the guy in the yellow raincoat could open the door. She would have time for two more on the walk back to work.

Agathe stamped out her final cigarette on the ground with the hundreds of others behind the building and kicked a plastic Coca-Cola bottle, bouncing it off the curb, before climbing up into the brownout of the loading dock.

By the time she reached the staff room, Agathe's eyes had adjusted to the darkness. She would go back to Hickey's next week. She blew into her hands, comforted by their friendly nicotine smell, and hung her coat and scarf on a hook. From the showroom, the honk of Tony's adoring laughter sang through the crack under the door, which meant Wood was telling a story.

"Espèce d'idiot," she muttered as she tied on her red smock and hurried for the stick of light under the door, not wanting to miss anything.

As she entered the showroom, Tony's posture stiffened slightly, and he acknowledged her with a nod of his already-bobbing head. Wood glanced in her direction and continued with his story.

"...and his fiancée was beautiful, you shoulda seen her. Easily ten years younger than me, but she was looking me up and down from the minute she walked in. Now, this was at a time when sound systems like this had just come out on the market and, y'know, not just everybody had one. Even in the city, only if you had serious cash did you even think of buying one of these babies. Everyone else was still listening to transistors. These things cost thousands of dollars and they were huge. Speakers up to the ceiling. If you had one, people came over to look at it as much as listen to it. So I'm showing them the model that's most popular for young couples, within what I've already established is their price range without even asking, and I can tell that—one—this guy is threatened by my comfort with a big stereo and—two—he knows his girl is checking me out and feels he has something to prove."

Wood paused for effect.

"The guy stops me in mid-pitch and asks what we have that's a little bigger, and I see him looking at the Rebirdo

TK3520. He looks from the Rebirdo to me, then back to the Rebirdo. His fiancée is looking from me to him to the stereo, back to him, back to me. I go over to the Rebirdo and lift the cover to the turntable. I check back over my shoulder at the guy. He doesn't flinch. I lift the tone arm so gently you'da thought it was a bomb, and I lay the stylus down on the album that's already in there, which is a Beethoven. Classy. I turn and face the two of them, and the music starts. The volume knob is only at one and the store windows are already buzzing. I go to crank it up to the next notch and I can tell the guy is scared. He can't handle the Rebirdo. So I turn it up to two. I can see in his eyes he's starting to panic, so I turn it up to three and the speakers are literally jumping off the floor. His fiancée isn't looking at him anymore, only at me and the TK3520. He knows he's lost. Without saying anything to her, he makes for the door and peels off in their station wagon. The fiancée comes over and stands right in front of me, looks me in the eye, and starts undoing my pants."

"No way," said Tony.

"I swear."

"So what did you do?"

"I screwed her brains out."

"Honk, honk. No way!"

"Lookit, that's what it was like in those days. I was getting it all the time—we all were. Being in stereo sales was like being an astronaut. The chicks were all over you. You were literally beating them off with a stick."

"Scusez là," said Agathe, stepping between the two of them and reaching just past Wood's face to a light fixture on the wall. Since she'd learned that Wood would never interrupt her cleaning, Agathe had started interrupting him by cleaning. It was the only shred of power she felt she

35

had there. "Crissement sale, cette lampe..." she said, taking out a J Cloth from her smock and rubbing at a spot on the mounting panel. She fussed with the cloth, folding it back up, before removing her arm from in front of Wood's face. He resumed, undeterred.

"Yep, knew what he was after the minute he walked in."

"Yeah," said Tony.

"Shoulda seen the guy, squealing out of the parking lot. Didn't know what he was in for that day, nossir."

"And you did it with his girlfriend?"

"I just said I did."

"Wow."

Agathe performed her own review at the same time, under her breath.

Lookit. You'da thought it was a bomb. Nossir.

Although Wood was an idiot, Agathe loved the way he talked. His stories were one of her primary means of absorbing English. She and Réjean had clung to their linguistic exclusivity as a point of honour. But without Réjean, Agathe was starting to enjoy the cowboy quality of English.

Tony and Wood had gone unnaturally silent, and Agathe looked up as the sliding-door sensor announced the arrival of a blond woman wearing a short skirt and a down-filled parka.

"Hi," she said loudly once inside, unzipping her coat. She glanced briefly around the store before asking, "Are you guys hiring?"

Agathe froze mid-dust.

Tony and Wood blinked and said nothing.

"Whaddyou do, sell things? Fix things? Sell things." The woman nodded.

There was a long pause, during which Agathe unintentionally took a step forward, before Wood said, "We, sell, things, that, people, bring, in, to, sell, to, us, yes."

"I used to be a cheerleader for the Valkyries. I can sell anything."

"...Mmn..." said Wood.

The woman laughed loudly—something between a scream and a cough—and said, "You don't believe me?"

Wood shook his head, then nodded.

The woman laughed again. "I'm Debbie," she said. "I'm busy this weekend, but I can start Monday. Is Monday okay?"

Wood said nothing.

"So, I'll see you Monday," she said.

Wood nodded.

"Wicked," said Debbie. "You won't regret it!" And she zipped up her parka and was gone, the sensor's electronic tone ringing in her wake.

Agathe watched as Debbie climbed into a white Honda Civic. She could already smell its fruity, smoky interior.

"Elle commence lundi?" she said.

"Yep," said Wood. "I think I'll give her a shot. Seems like a nice kid."

They stood in silence until Tony turned to Wood and said, "I think she really liked you."

Wood Debow, Stereoblast branch manager, had been pursuing the Branch of the Year Award for a decade, and Agathe was part of his new Shiny-Makes-It-Sell strategy. The newest challenge issued by Head Office was for each branch to reduce overhead by any means possible, with rewards for the most creative ideas. Wood's solution was darkness. He cut the electricity bill in half by installing bulbs with less than half the required wattage in some staff areas, while in others he dispensed with them altogether. Agathe locked up and ran the Shop-Vac over the industrial carpet at night by the low-pressure sodium light from the parking lot. Someone had brought in the Shop-Vac a few years ago to sell, the carpet brush bound to the end of the hose with a thickness of hockey tape. Though functional, it couldn't be sold. The owner had left it behind nonetheless, and Wood had put it straight into the Possibility Pile outside his office. He never knew when he might need an appliance that partially worked.

In the dark, Agathe could only gauge the effectiveness of her vacuuming by sound. A gritty clicking told her something was getting sucked up the hose, but the carpet never got clean. And it didn't matter, because Wood would never mention the carpet not getting clean, because it would mean admitting he should buy a new vacuum, which would exceed the budget. So Agathe turned on the Shop-Vac every night to move it cautiously around the floor, keeping an eye out for movement in the darkened store. The layout of the high metal shelves provided perfect concealment for murderers, and the noise of the vacuum, moreover, ensured that Agathe would never hear them sneaking up behind her until it was too late. She felt it was just a matter of time.

Around Halloween, just after Agathe had started working there, Wood began defining his energy-saving policy. He scanned his internal database for free things he could use for promotional purposes, shuffling options for one that could be integrated with the theme of darkness. This led him to his brother Garvey's pest-control company. Around the fall, bats would start looking for warm places to spend the winter, and the Victorian homes in the area had big, empty attics for hibernation. Garvey got a lot of bat calls.

Wood thought darkness, he thought energy conservation, he thought daylight savings, he thought Halloween, he thought bats, he thought vermin: he thought mascot. Not only was the bat a creature of curiosity that many people didn't get to see close-up, it also thrived in the dark. It was perfect. A bat on display was outrageous enough to get the attention of Head Office, but was also absolutely free and employed a resource whose alternative fate was release into the wild, from which no one profited.

Wood unveiled the bat one morning from beneath one of Agathe's dusting cloths (she wondered how he knew where to find one), and Tony said "Wow" before the large-dome birdcage had been revealed.

"This little guy," Wood announced, "is going to make us some money. I put an ad in the paper. A bat? In an electronics store? *At Halloween?* They're gonna be flooding in."

Tony reached for his hair.

Agathe craned forward to get a look. Hanging upside down from the perch was a fat brown bat with big, pointy ears. He had a swiney, pushed-in nose and bewildered eyes, which he set instantly on Agathe.

"Aie, ce n'est pas un oiseau, là," she said.

"That's right, Agathe, it's not," said Wood. "What it is, is a sales technique. A bat? In a cage? In an electronics store? C'mon! You show me another retail outlet that's tried it. You can't. Because they haven't."

Agathe turned to the bat. "Ce soir," she said, making a flapping motion in the air with her hand.

Tony asked if they could name the bat Atrius. He had been in a band in high school called Atrium, but Atrius was what he'd always wished they'd called themselves. He loved the sound of it. *Atrius*. Like a rock god.

Atrius slept for most of the day, except the moments when Agathe looked over to find his frightened eyes on her. She nodded back in assurance and watched as the customers, one after another, approached his cage and turned away, confused. They knew. They knew bats didn't belong in cages—in broad daylight. But nobody said anything.

At closing time, Wood passed Atrius on his way to the door and chuckled one last time, shaking his head.

"Bat..." he said.

Agathe locked up with Atrius watching her, unblinking. When she approached the cage, he fluttered his wings, clutching the perch upside down. She reached for the latch, then thought of the rafters. She should take him outside, so she wasn't chasing him around with the broom. A bat couldn't use the automatic door.

The cage was dangling from a stand that suspended Atrius at eye level. When Agathe lifted the pedestal, the unexpected weight displacement caused the cage to tilt, releasing it from the hook and sending it rolling across the floor. She hurried over, waving her hands, "Je m'excuse," she whispered. "Je m'excuse."

He'd been knocked from the perch and was struggling to right himself and untangle his wings. When she crouched down to pick him up and her shadow fell over him, he turned upward to face her, his eyes wide, and began frantically beating his wings against the bars.

"Non, non," she said, and pointed at the front doors, but he wouldn't look at the front doors. She leaned in again and went to put her hands on either side of the cage, but he started flapping so hard, she took her hands away and held them up to show him.

"Voyons," she said. "Ce n'est que moi." He suddenly flew at the bars, pushing his face against them, biting, his lips curled back in a horrible hiss. Something had changed in him. There was none of the softness in the eyes that had watched her all day. Now he looked angry. He looked like he wanted to bite her.

She sat back on her heels and watched him thrash. If she released him now, he'd swoop right up and bite her face. She sucked in her breath, pinched the loop of the cage from the floor without touching the rest, and dropped it back on the hook.

He was shaking his head like a dog, baring his teeth, hissing. It was then she remembered the raccoon in the back garden when she was a girl, and her father with a brick and a pillowcase. La rage. He'd ordered her back inside, but she remembered the teeth.

The more she watched Atrius pitch and hiss, the clearer it became that she couldn't let him go.

Surely Garvey had dealt with bats in this state. Surely he could take it back and release it where it would be safe.

The wail of the Shop-Vac drowned out the leathery flapping of his wings, but she felt his eyes on her back.

The next morning, Atrius lay curled up in the bottom of his cage, blinking. His eyes sought Agathe as she, Tony, and Wood gathered around.

"Dammit," said Wood. "We're going to need another bat." And he called Garvey.

Agathe looked into Atrius's eyes, the same gentle ones that had followed her all day yesterday. He wasn't snarling or agitated. Just finished. He had flapped himself out.

"Well, why didn't you say so?" Wood shouted into the telephone. "Sonofabitch," he announced after he'd hung up. "Turns out you're not supposed to put 'em in cages. Kills 'em. We'd have to get a new bat every few days. Sonofabitch."

Tony went to hoist the cage and take it out back, but Agathe put her hand on his arm.

"Non," she said. "C'est fragile."

Out on the loading dock, she unhooked the cage from the stand, sat down on the smoking bench, and rested Atrius in her lap. He was rolled over to one side with his toes curled up. She caressed the metal bars and closed her eyes. "Je m'excuse," she said. She lifted the latch of the door and opened it to the sky. Atrius blinked.

She sat with him a while longer, rocking him in her lap. When she finally had to go inside, she set his cage in the sunny spot by the door.

Tony came in with the empty cage a few hours later and brought it down to the Possibility Pile.

From then on, Atrius was her burden every night in the dark, with the Shop-Vac and his little ghost.

THEN

Martin had been writing up his daily sales report when there was a knock on the door of the portable. Réjean entered without saying a word, sat down in his chair, and heaved a sigh that Martin could only read as a plea for inquiry. He gingerly put down his pen.

Réjean was spinning around in his chair, arms hanging limply at his sides, head back, gazing at the ceiling like a teenager. Martin couldn't sound out whether he was ready to share or not. Réjean had been distracted lately, and Martin struggled with the desire to ask him about it, but worried about crippling the friendship with inappropriate closeness or upsetting its balance in any way.

"C'est une crise, Martin," said Réjean at last.

Martin had never had an easy time with men. He grew up painfully observing the rapport between his father, Jack Bureau, his brothers, Derek and Troy, and Jack's omni-present companion and next-door neighbour, Roy Doake, when they would assemble in the basement for one of their Meetings.

Meetings were understood to be for the purpose of grown-up men to address pressing issues. Martin knew, of course, that they were for goofing off and drinking rum. Lamb's Navy. Theirs was a cousinage de plaisanterie, where custom rendered every man free to tease the other past the point of civility, with immunity for none, and no right to feeling hurt. But the fun was not extended to Martin. He felt his exclusion so acutely, it was incredible no one mentioned it.

More than anything, Martin wanted to be invited to one of his father's Meetings. But it never happened. Jack died at dinner one Sunday while Roy and the entire family looked on. A hunk of steak lodged in his esophagus took him down in a few stifled breaths. Martin would never know the communion of a rum with his dad. Nor would he let Réjean know how much their friendship filled that need.

Martin grasped the arms of his chair and pulled himself upright. He hesitated for a moment, reached for the desk drawer, and grabbed the Lamb's. He spilled some as he poured two healthy-sized drinks and, steadying himself, held one out to Réjean.

"Okay," he said. And they drank.

Réjean started with a slow exhale out his nose that whistled through his moustache.

"Ben, Martin, trop c'est easy, ma vie. Tout est là, mais y'a un thing qui manque...J'sais pas."

"Okay, something's missing," confirmed Martin once he felt he had given Réjean sufficient time.

Réjean nodded, then shook his head, then shrugged and said, "Beunh."

Martin sat back. Réjean was looking for a suggestion. Martin felt he was in over his head, but he had to say something and it had to be good. He imagined offering such helpful advice to Réjean that perhaps Réjean would one day attribute his happiness to Martin's sage counsel.

"What do you do in your spare time?" he asked. "When you're not working or eating or sleeping."

"Ben, je drive mon truck."

"Okay, yes. Do you go to the movies? Do you read books?"

Réjean thought for a long time and said, "Beunh," again. "Non."

"Collect anything?"

"Non."

Martin thought about his own hobby: the squeal of mud under the tires of the Ranger, the exhilaration of speed and abandon. How it picked him up when he was down, how his enjoyment of off-roading solidified him as a person, made him less inconsistent and lost. But he also thought of how hard he had to work at hiding the brand he drove: parking his truck in a lot four blocks from the dealership, telling the guys he didn't even own a vehicle, that he took the bus, because of the price of gas. It was heavy enough to carry around, but not being able to talk about his truck with Réjean made it unbearable. If anyone would understand, it would be Réjean.

"What do you find fun?" asked Martin.

Réjean thought seriously about it. He hid a smile as he pictured the game he and Agathe had played the night before, where he pretended to be her little brother, climbing into her bed seeking comfort after a nightmare. She gave him a kind of fun he would never have dreamed possible, and the idea of needing something else made him feel wretched.

"Ben, Agathe," said Réjean. And after a moment, "Et mon truck."

Martin was winging it, but considering the grievances he had heard from the other sales guys about money and ex-wives, Réjean's troubles seemed minor. He wondered if the solution could be so painless. He sat back in his chair and assessed Réjean for a moment. "A man needs a hobby," he said, with increasing confidence, "to make him feel alive."

Réjean swivelled in his chair toward the window, taking these in as exactly the words he needed. "Un hobby..." he said, turning slowly back to Martin. "Oui! Je vais adopter un hobby."

Martin blasted the French folk station as the windshield wipers sloshed against the pelting rain. Édith Butler was singing to him about Paquetville, which sounded like a lovely place.

This weather was perfect, producing the kind of slippery muck he really needed. He was wearing his yellow rain gear—coat, pants with suspenders, and sou'wester—standard apparel for Martin when he went off-roading. He hated getting wet, but more importantly he hated getting dirty.

Martin had learned the joys of off-road trucking from his dad. Jack Bureau had owned a towing and snow-removal business and would be called upon whenever a truck got stuck. Because he thought they'd find it fun, Jack began bringing Troy and Derek along on foul-weather tows, instilling in them an early appreciation of trucks and towing. It was agreed that Martin was too young and didn't go in for that anyway. But whenever Jack got the call, Martin wanted desperately to be asked along. One day, the Pattersons' station wagon got stuck in the front ditch, and as Derek and Troy grabbed their jackets, Martin appeared in the kitchen doorway, dressed in his rain gear. Jack hesitated only briefly before leading him out the door.

Parked in front of the Pattersons' house, Martin watched, squashed between Troy and Derek, as his father hitched up the truck to the distressed wagon. When they were yanked back in their seats at the first victorious jerk, Derek and

Troy hooted and hollered, while Martin beamed inwardly at the thrill of being in the fray.

When the job was done, Jack Bureau drove them to a nearby field and they howled with laughter, Martin included, as he drove doughnuts in the mud, the wet cows chewing disinterestedly in their direction. It was the most fun Martin had ever had.

Jack Bureau used only Ford trucks on the job. They were a strong, imposing vehicle, with a reputation for reliability in any climate and superior towing capacity. Just as Martin had learned from his dad that it was a man's responsibility to provide for his family and stand by his friends, he learned that the Ford embodied all that was right and true.

Losing his father cemented Martin's allegiance to the Ford brand. He vowed that in his honour, he would never drive anything but a Ford. The circumstances of his hiring by the Chevy dealership were something he couldn't help. He hoped that if his father were still around, he would forgive his working for a competitor.

Martin's enjoyment of an afternoon off-roading in the Ranger was a tribute to his father, and it had brought him nothing but joy until the day he met Réjean. As their friendship matured and their bond through the Chevy brand was galvanized, Martin's secret grew more and more burdensome.

Jack Bureau would never lie to Roy about the brand of truck he drove. Martin tried to rationalize it by convincing himself that it was a different friendship. He and Réjean would never have what Jack and Roy had, by virtue of Réjean's happy home life. He knew that Réjean wouldn't pass over Agathe for any man, the way Jack and Roy put each other before their own wives. He decided that if Réjean had a right to live in a world that didn't include him, so he could not be held to live by Réjean's vehicular preference. Part of him felt righteous about this and part of him knew that secrets had no place in a friendship. He tried to keep the righteous part closer to the front. But once he reached a good, muddy stretch of ground, he found he was able to clear his mind and indulge completely in the pleasure of the Ranger's wheels churning through the muck.

NOW

Agathe had coiled the cord around the Shop-Vac and was locking the front door when the bus appeared over the crest of the hill, promising swift delivery home to Friday night, the best and worst night of the week—two days away from Stereoblast, but two days alone in the empty house, watching for Réjean to walk through the door. She never ran for the bus, but tonight she felt so overwhelmed by the need to get home that she launched forward and sprinted for the stop, puffing, waving frantically at the driver. The bus hissed as it slowed down and she slapped her hand against its side, wheezing.

The remoteness of the cottage along the rural route meant that by the time Agathe reached her stop, she was usually the only passenger remaining on the bus. It gave her a lot of time to think, sitting in the very back, watching the road stretch farther and farther away from Stereoblast. Every so often, her heart would jump at the sight of a passing Silverado, though not the way it once did. The Silverado was, of course, home in the garage. Waiting.

She stepped down from the bus and onto the blackened stretch of gravel that led home.

At the front door, she felt the familiar thrill at seeing the thick brown envelope from the market research company on the doorstep. Sondage didn't arrive with the other mail; it was delivered special, just for her. She picked up the envelope, set it down on the table, and rushed to make a pot of tea.

Not long after Agathe started at Stereoblast, she had been lighting her first cigarette outside the front doors of Hickey's when a young man approached her, looking for committed smokers. When he asked Agathe her daily intake, she thought seriously before responding.

"Vingt-huit?" She didn't want to put herself out of the running if there was a prize—particularly if it was free cigarettes. And it was. Participants were asked to smoke three packs of test cigarettes and rate their smoking satisfaction as compared to their usual brand. At first, Sondage asked Agathe questions pertaining directly to smoking: how did she feel about the taste, aftertaste, harshness, aesthetic appeal, smoke production, burn speed, length, duration, lingering effects in the throat and lungs, smell (while burning and on the breath afterwards), packaging, and overall enjoyment of the test cigarettes? She didn't normally think about the individual components of smoking and found it compelling to fully immerse herself into the analysis of an activity she adored.

The final question of the survey asked, How do you feel about cigarettes? She responded: Je les aime. Elles sont mes amies.

From that time, she and Sondage had been building a friendship that gave her something to look forward to, occupied her mind, and made her feel close to happiness. As they grew closer, Sondage began asking more and more intimate questions. *Why don't you wear more red? Is anyone being cruel to you?* Agathe would think seriously about her responses all day at work, then try and phrase them like a story she wanted Sondage to hear, in the survey's General Comments section.

She poured her tea, sat at the kitchen table, and lit the first of the new test cigarettes. She found it much trop fort and checked box number one. She often found the sample cigarettes *trop fort*. The cigarette companies seemed to be always working on a stronger cigarette. If she couldn't smoke them, she wondered who could.

She flipped to the back page and ran her hand over the empty sky blue of the General Comments box. She hovered the tip of her pen over the top left-hand corner of the box, then moved it down to the centre of the page. She hadn't drawn a picture since Réjean had gone. Without making contact, she began circling the tip of the pen around and around, the side of her hand shooshing against the paper, until she stopped and cautiously drew a circle, closing it up at the top where it had begun. From there, she drew a series of wild squiggles ventilating out beyond the edges of the box. She pulled herself in closer to the table, rested both elbows, and brought her nose down to the page as she worked. When she sat back, Debbie stood tall as a skyscraper, shrieking with laughter as she breathed fire out both nostrils, setting ablaze a tiny Wood and Tony, who trembled beneath her. As they screamed and crackled, she lifted her blue pump and crushed them out like cigarettes. In the background, Agathe drew herself, a circle and two sticks, sitting at the wheel of a truck, ready to peel out of the Stereoblast parking lot, headed for the city. She had captured Debbie, even if it looked nothing like her: the nimbus of hair, the sporty parka. But what pleased her most was the accuracy of Debbie's laugh: a set of radiant lines, a tuba, and a housefly.

Agathe had just started running the bathwater to wash away the week when it struck her to pull out her other drawing, the one she hadn't looked at since Réjean had gone. From between the mattress and box spring, she pulled the bloc-notes and brought it to the kitchen table. But as she opened it up to the page with her anniversary drawing, a wave of darkness washed over her and she had to close it. Too fast. She took a breath and opened it again, trying to look at it simply as a thing. She turned her head sideways and contemplated it, then turned the page sideways and brought her head upright. It was so good, she had a hard time believing it was her own. She propped it up on the table and stood all the way back to the doorway, then through the doorway into the living room. The perspective was perfect, and the white spaces she'd left white actually looked like shiny reflections. She ran down for the empty frame in the basement and pressed her drawing into the mat. She took down the calendar filled with the days of Réjean's absence, and hung up her drawing. Arms folded, she stood in the living room doorway as down the hall the bathwater crept past the overflow drain.

THEN

Réjean thought a lot about Martin's suggestion. He devoted so much time to it, in fact, that it started to distract him from his home life. He would disconnect from Agathe and disappear into his mind, where he tried to come up with a suitable hobby. He had the physical power of three or four men and enjoyed being the guy people called when a tree needed to be moved off a trapped co-worker or someone needed to reach something high up. He was also grateful for his size when he saw the light that brightened Agathe's sometimes-sad face as he whisked her off her feet and spun her around in the kitchen. He loved being a big man. Perhaps his hobby could incorporate his size.

Because he was generally content and even-tempered, he had never gotten angry enough to want to inflict the harm of which he was capable. Violence was bad and it would disappoint Agathe, but years of being treated with the deference of men had made him curious to see what they so feared.

He closed his eyes one day while he was out in the woods and tried to picture what it would feel like to fully exert his force upon a deserving target, but could not come up with sufficient cause. He tried to think of something that made him so angry that the only imaginable recourse would be the unleashing of violence, but found it impossible to fully immerse himself in a fantasy without absolute verisimilitude. His fantasies had to be feasible within his world, and the most hatefully realistic image he could summon up—

the most repulsive and rage-inducing tableau conceivable—was of another man forcing himself on Agathe. Réjean's body began to pulse with fury the moment it occurred to him. The attacker would be from the city, with long yellow hair and a moustache, Réjean decided—but not a thick, sensuous one like his own. It would be thin and manicured, extending down into a thin, manicured beard, a style of facial hair worn by men Réjean considered untrustworthy. The man would wear a leather jacket and leather pants with heavy, buckled boots. He would be rugged, but arrogantly fashionable. Réjean hated him.

He pictured the man pulling up to the driveway in a dirty Ford F-100 during the morning while Réjean was at work, parking it under the trees near the road. In the fantasy, Agathe was at the counter rolling out dough for one of her meat pies, wearing a velour track suit, the kind she'd taken to wearing since her midsection had begun to expand. The top of the man's head appeared at the kitchen window, revealing his receding hairline, then the ungroomed brows, then the eyes that locked on Agathe as she kneaded the floured pastry. His head disappeared from the window, and the knob of the front door turned so quietly she could not hear it over her own humming. He entered the kitchen and stood still for a moment, just breathing, drawing excitement from being undetected. He moved slowly, speeding up as he reached her, grabbing her with one hand over her mouth, his other arm holding her middle section just as she turned at the sound of him. She tried to scream, but only made a muffled sound with her nose. Her eyes rolled left and right as she tried to get a look at him. In his mind, Réjean saw the big kitchen knife on the counter, but Agathe was too shocked to think to use it. The man's hand moved up to her breasts and caressed them in a taunting way as he whispered ugly words to her in English. Then he flung her from standing at the counter to lying spread-eagle, face down on the kitchen table. Agathe squirmed on the table, and the man grabbed her hands, leaving her legs free to kick the air. He became angry at her resistance and turned her on her back and shook her until she lay still and sobbed under his hand. He brought his terrible moustache close to her face and grunted as he fumbled with the top of her pants. Agathe's face was streaked with tears as she peered toward the kitchen window, seeking help in the thick pines outside.

This was the moment Réjean pulled up in the Silverado, having realized at work that he had forgotten his tool belt on the bedside table after a game they'd played the night before. For the sake of realism, his mind flashed to an image of his tool belt next to the reading lamp. He slowed down as he approached the driveway and knew from the Ford parked on the road that something was wrong.

He made for the front door with a few strides of his massive legs, and through the window his eyes connected with Agathe's, which filled with relief. He punched the door right off its hinges and it crashed down on the kitchen floor, startling the attacker. He grabbed the man by the back of his leather jacket, pulled him off Agathe, spun him around, and drove his head and shoulders into the wall. The man fell to the floor, and Réjean stood over him, pressing his boot down on the attacker's chest. He spat on the man before picking him up and swinging him around the kitchen by his boots, smashing his head into the door frame. The man's face poured blood and he was losing consciousness. Having no desire to torture him, but only to employ every ounce of his strength in pulverizing him, Réjean continued smashing the man's head against the door frame until it popped right off.

It was at this moment that Réjean opened his eyes, his pulse racing and every nerve in his body tingling. He closed his eyes again to resume the dream as he released his grip on the attacker's feet. The man's heavy, leather-clad body thumped to the floor, and Réjean stepped out of the way so as not to get blood on his workboots. Agathe leaped into his arms and he held her close. She cried and laughed, touching his face, and he held hers in his hands as he kissed the tracks of her tears.

He had never felt so alive.

More and more often, Réjean pulled over to the side of the highway on his way home from work to indulge in his hobby. Behind the wheel of the Silverado was the place he most enjoyed daydreaming. He sometimes lost himself so completely that when he opened his eyes, he was late for dinner and had to make up an excuse. He hated lying to Agathe and vowed each time to be more careful. He tried not to practise his hobby while he was at home, but sometimes in bed, while Agathe was lying asleep in his armpit, he would drift off into vivid reveries of her attack and squeeze her so hard she would wake up. He would tell her he dreamed he was falling.

One night, he stopped in at a service station to fill up the Silverado. When he went inside to pay, two men were standing ahead of him at the cash, disputing with the attendant. They looked like they were from the city. One was big and bald with a bushy red beard, and the other had a mane of curly golden hair, on top of which sat a cowboy hat. Both of them wore leather jackets and cowboy boots. The service station didn't carry their brand of cigarettes and they were loudly attributing the oversight to small-town ignorance. They asked what, of the shit the store did carry, might be similar to their brand. The attendant replied that he was sorry, but he didn't know because he didn't smoke. The men laughed uproariously and turned to solicit Réjean's participation. They had to crane their necks to find his face above them and when they did, Réjean saw the blond man's thin, manicured beard. They went quiet as he focused his attention on the man's face. The man turned, politely ordered any old brand of cigarettes, and paid for their gas. As they waited for their change, Réjean stepped forward, reached out a finger, and nudged up the back brim of the blond man's hat so that the front covered his eyes. When he saw the man's shoulders stiffen, Réjean paused, and then, with languorous precision, continued tipping the brim of the hat upward until it flipped off the man's head and landed face up on the counter with a *floof*.

The bald man made for the door. Réjean heard an engine starting up in the parking lot, and the blond man stood rigidly, looking down at his hat. He reached slowly for his cigarettes and took a tentative step sideways, then another, until he was out of Réjean's reach, and then broke into a run, leaving the hat and his change.

Réjean paid the grateful attendant, shrugged, said, "Beunh," and picked up the hat.

In the driveway at home, he put on the hat and cocked it before getting out of the truck. When Agathe opened the door, he plopped it on her head, and while the mashed potatoes browned on top of a shepherd's pie in the oven, they played a cowgirl game where she tied him to one of the kitchen chairs.

After the gas station, Réjean became bolder. The feeling of his own dominance exhilarated him, and public places became fertile ground for his new hobby. He had stopped to pick up a can of coffee on his way home from work when a dirty brown Ford F-100 squealed into the lot and pulled in right next to him, loudly playing rock and roll music. His heart sped up. The windows of the truck were rolled halfway down, because the exposed glass was too dirty to see out of. The driver turned off the engine but remained in the truck, singing along to the guitar solo.

Weow, weow, weow, meeoh, weeeeeeeeeeeeoh.

When the song faded out, Réjean watched cautiously as the man stepped down from the cab. He was an army man, wearing a camouflage jacket and pants. He was big, but not as big as Réjean. He headed into the store, drumming his thighs. Réjean hated the man's choice of music, but what really got him was the truck. He sat for a moment until it overcame him, and as calmly as he could with all the adrenaline flowing through his veins, he walked around to the driver-side door, licked his finger, and underneath the window wrote, *LAVE-MOI*.

He felt this to be a badge of the deepest shame. How could anyone let their vehicle get so dirty—even if it *was* a Ford? He climbed back into the Silverado, rolled down his window and tried to calm his heart as he waited for the man's return. When the man reappeared carrying a box of cereal, he slowed down, absorbing the offence. He looked up through the two sets of rolled-down windows, and into Réjean's eyes. He looked hurt, but not the least bit afraid. He had a sympathetic and admittedly handsome face, with a fine, slender nose and elegantly turned nostrils. It was a face that had been so carefree just moments ago when he pulled into the lot. This left Réjean with the difficult decision of what to do with his own face. The man's lack of fear made him writhe. Perhaps if the man could see the size of him, it would solve things, so Réjean opened the door and unfolded his legs from the cab, dangling them for effect before letting his boots touch the ground. He stretched his long, long arms so the man could take him in, and strolled on into the store, feeling the man's eyes follow him closely. From inside the store, he glanced out the window to find the Ford gone.

There was a cloud of regret obscuring his enjoyment. He had never felt like a bully before. There had been no reason to provoke the man, and now *LAVE-MOI* didn't strike him as clever at all, but a cruel and unwarranted assault on another man's vehicle—particularly someone who had devoted himself to the protection of their country's freedom. Agathe would be disappointed. He climbed back into the Silverado and headed home, knowing she would want to play a pretending game when he got there, reminding himself how little he deserved it.

NOW

Tony's and Wood's laughter roared from the showroom Monday morning as Agathe tied on her smock, and in its midst, one unmistakable brassy blond cackle.

Agathe held her breath. She slipped into the showroom to see the backs of Tony and Wood and the front of Debbie, who was seated on the corner of a display table in a miniskirt, eating pudding out of a container with her finger. Wood's hair was wet. Agathe headed straight for the consoles at the back. Tony nodded, spellbound, as Debbie continued.

"So at halftime, I'm just about to go out back with the girls for a drink behind the bleachers and Becky taps me on the shoulder and says this guy is trying to get my attention. So I look and there's this executive CEO-type guy waving at me from the front row of seats, and I go 'Me?' and he's nodding, so I go over and he says that he's had his eye on me for a few games now and asks if I want to go and watch the game from up the Executive Box, 'coz, he says a girl like me deserves nice things. He says they have some *thing* up there, and I say, I don't even know what that is, and he says it's some kind of expensive champagne and that he's never seen a cheerleader as pretty as me."

The air hummed.

"So I tell the girls I'm going with this guy, and they're all like, 'Oh my god.' The game is like twelve to zero and people are leaving at halftime anyway. So we go up the Executive Box, which is this swanky room with wood panelling and couches and it looks over the field and so there's buckets filled with ice and all kinds of beer and wine and that champagne with the name I don't know and so he opens a bottle of that and I ask for a beer. So I'm sitting on his lap on the couch and he's telling me about his wife and how they never do it and how they haven't done it since they had their last kid (who's nine) and I'm like, 'You poor baby.' So the game is still going on and I say, 'Do you want to see a trick?'"

Agathe stopped her duster in mid-fluff.

"So there's this trick I can do where I drink a whole beer, bottle or can, without using my hands, and not spill a drop. So I go over to the cooler and get another beer and open it and I straddle him on the couch and I put the beer between my tits and lean back. And I'm drinking and he's laughing, and so my head is almost between my heels and then I fall right off the couch onto the floor. I got Schooner all over my mink. It was hilarious."

Debbie laughed, Tony laughed a moment after, Wood opened his mouth, but nothing came out, and Agathe wandered to the next planter, murmuring, "*Schooner all over my mink...*"

Debbie tossed her pudding container in the garbage as the door sensor went *bing bing* and a young couple dragged in a set of big wooden speakers and a stereo. Debbie clicked over to greet them.

"Whaddya got there?" she asked, wrapping her arms around the console the man held. A little startled by her nearness, he told her it was a Rebirdo TK3520 and a set of Mandios. He and his wife had gotten them as a wedding gift ten years ago and were looking to upgrade, but the equipment was in perfect working order.

"Let's have a look," Debbie said, lugging the console across the floor to a power outlet. The man and woman briskly picked up a speaker each and followed her. She plugged the stereo into the test outlet and from behind the unit said, "I'll bet the red wire goes into this red notchy thing and the black one goes into the black notchy thing…"

She came around to the front, crouched down, and turned on the power. The sound of a talk-radio announcer embroiled in a heated exchange with a caller came from the right speaker. Wood and Tony looked on in reserved awe, as did the husband. His wife rolled her eyes.

"Your left speaker's broken, sweetheart," said Debbie from the floor.

"Yeah, sorry. Right," he said.

"Okay, I'll give you twenty bucks for the whole thing," Debbie said, straightening up and tugging her skirt back down.

"Twenty!"

"Nobody uses these components anymore, hon, and you have a busted left speaker. We'll be lucky if we can sell these at all. But you can certainly take them somewhere else and see if they'll buy them."

"There's nowhere else in town."

Debbie shrugged and smiled, laying a twenty-dollar bill from the register on the counter and draping her breasts over her folded arms. The man grabbed the twenty from the counter and nearly ran out of the store. His wife followed him with ominous languor.

Agathe thought her heart would fly out her mouth.

"Do you have a screwdriver?" asked Debbie, back behind the speakers.

"What?" said Wood.

"You have to take these apart to get to the insides," she said, "and I'm gonna need a screwdriver."

"We, I—no, I don't know," said Wood. "No. We wouldn't. Why would we?"

Debbie began rifling through a drawer and instantly produced a screwdriver. She crouched down on her hands and knees and started turning the screws on the back of the speaker. She looked for a minute at the insides, then reached in and pulled out two wires covered in yellow plastic. She picked at them with her nails until a split formed in the covering, peeled it back to expose the naked wires, twisted them around each other, and hit the radio switch again. The sound of the quarrel between the announcer and caller belted forth loudly with perfect clarity from both speakers, one carrying the announcer, the other the caller. Debbie reached for the dial and switched it decisively to the right. The moment her fingers released it, the speakers declared that now they were messing with a sonofabitch.

"Hell yeah," said Debbie, bobbing her head with the cowbell.

Tony's mouth hung shamelessly ajar while Wood crossed—then uncrossed—his arms.

Euphoria surged through Agathe, radiating from her soul to the tips of her hair. It was rock and roll, wholly personified in Debbie.

Debbie mussed her hair back into place and said, "I'm going out for a smoke." Then to Agathe, "Wanna come?"

"Ben oui!" said Agathe.

"I..." said Wood.

"For every two and a half hours we work," said Tony, "we get fifteen minutes. Then half an hour at lunch. We shouldn't really have a break until ten-thirty."

"I have an addiction." Debbie beamed and spun on her heels toward the staff room.

Debbie was a sonofabitch.

Debbie stood on the loading dock, smoking in her down-filled parka. The scar on her chin made a little dimple as she smiled at Agathe. "So how long have you worked here?" Debbie asked.

"Six mois," said Agathe.

"How do you stand it with those guys?" she asked. "Jesus."

Agathe laughed. "Ben c'est un show, là," she said. "Ça passe de time."

They stood in silence for a moment, Debbie exhaling like a queen, nodding.

"Do you like to party?" asked Debbie.

Agathe nodded vigorously. "Ah oui, oui." Whatever it was, she was sure she'd love it.

"We should go out sometime. Tear the place up."

THEN

Martin had been thinking about a rum when Réjean appeared at the door to the portable on Monday just before quitting time.

"Hey!" Martin said, reaching for the bottle in the desk drawer, "I was just..." But he stopped when Réjean dropped into the grey wool chair, his great hands dangling between his legs.

Martin quietly poured them a drink.

"Mon hobby," Réjean said at last, to the floor.

A long silence followed.

"Ça ne va pas," said Réjean.

"Okay," said Martin cautiously.

Réjean took a deep breath and a slug of rum. He told Martin how he'd been standing at the Lobster Shack counter and had looked down the hill to the parking lot to see the man in the very truck on which he'd written *LAVE-MOI* pointing and shouting at Agathe. The man had threatened her and she was terrified, and it was all Réjean's fault. Because he was crazy, the army man was not afraid of Réjean, therefore there was no telling what he might do next. Réjean didn't want to hurt the man; he only wanted to scare him back, to stop him. He rolled himself up to Martin's desk and looked him in the eye.

"Martin, j'ai besoin d'un gun."

Martin let the words play over in his head, reached out again for the bottle, and slowly poured them another drink.

If Roy had needed a gun, Jack Bureau would have gotten it for him no matter what. This was what you did for a friend.

Cautious of overpromising (Underpromise, overdeliver—the golden rule of sales) he told Réjean to leave it with him.

The next morning, Martin gave a final squeeze to the tissues in his pocket and walked into the showroom while the guys were having coffee. He didn't drink coffee because it made him sweat, but right now he needed to fit in. He selected a mug that read *Super Dad* and poured himself a cup, dumping in four packets of sugar.

A few weeks back, while the sales guys were having coffee, Steve Addison had been telling a story about his neighbour, an old Polish woman, who believed the fence separating their yards was twenty-eight inches shy of the property line on her side. This entitled her, she claimed, to twenty-eight inches of Addison's yard. She would avail herself of these inches of Addison's manicured lawn as a repository for her garbage. Now she was having work done on the house and those inches had become the dumping site for all her renovation waste. Addison had tried everything, but there was no reasoning with her. He had never met anyone so tenacious. She was not swayed by threats of legal action, rightly convinced as she was that Steve couldn't be bothered to take her to court. In desperation, Steve tried threatening her physically, but she had spent two years in a concentration camp during WWII and managed to escape by digging under a fence with her hands. She feared nothing, least of all Steve Addison. She was also in excellent health and looked like she'd be around for a while.

One of the guys had said, "Looks like you're going to have to pay a visit to Colonel Weed," and they had all chuckled.

Martin hadn't asked what was funny, because that was how he usually ruined people's jokes.

Now he sidled over with his *Super Dad* mug, trying so hard to think of a subtle way to broach the topic that when Ferris, the new guy, said, "Good morning," Martin replied, "Who's Colonel Weed?"

The guys looked at each other and there was a long moment while each of them waited for someone else to respond.

"He's a...he's a...he's a bit of a bad guy," said Steve. "He's like a guy you call when you need things. Like bad things."

"I need something," said Martin, the veins in his forehead pulsing.

The guys liked Martin, but they didn't understand him. He took the bus to work. It just didn't make sense. They laughed at him when he was serious and took him literally when he was joking. But something about his strained voice assured them this wasn't supposed to be funny.

The guys, in fact, knew very little about the Colonel, except that he was extremely dangerous. There was some hushed lore about him, but none of them knew anyone who'd met him face to face. He lived in the woods, they said, outside of town, past the turnoff to the old Presbyterian church with the sign facing the wrong way, and you had to walk through the woods, without a flashlight, until you found him. And you didn't find him, the guys said—he found you.

In his portable after work that night, he steeled himself with a rum, then another rum, waiting for daylight to fade. He was not cut out for dangerous things. He had never in his life been in a situation like this and had no idea how he would respond to danger. He wished there were a way to turn off his nervousness just for a little while. He thought about the way dogs attacked when they sensed fear. Surely the Colonel wouldn't interpret his nervousness as a threat.

He mentally recited the directions in French to calm himself.

"Suivez la route 11 jusqu'au parking lot du traversier. Tournez à droite. Continuez sur le 11 jusqu'à l'ensigne pour l'église presbytérienne."

He would have to walk through the woods, which meant getting his shoes dirty. The sweat factory was running on all pistons as he sat at his desk. He would be soaked by the time he got there, and tissues would not cover this level of nervousness. It was four blocks to the lot where he parked the Ranger, then the drive to the church would take approximately forty-five minutes, time enough, he hoped, to dry off in the truck with the fan.

The sky over the lot went yellow, then pink, then purple.

"L'heure est arrivée," he told himself.

When Martin was a boy and a towing call would come in, Jack Bureau would throw on his quilted vest before he had even hung up the phone, grab his keys, kiss Mrs. Bureau, and start the truck all before his other arm had slid into its armhole. Martin tried to do the same now by downing the rest of his rum and throwing on his jacket, tearing the lining. He wanted nothing more than to stay here in the office and drink rum, but there was no way he couldn't try to help his friend. He cast a last look down at Réjean's chair as he closed the door.

In the Ranger, the fan on full bore, he reminded himself not to talk too much. Soyez normal, he thought. Soyez normal. He would come and go as unremarkably as he could.

He held his palms up to the fan one at a time, then assured himself that if he did make it in to see Colonel Weed, handshaking was unlikely.

"Il fait noir," he said. "Il y a beaucoup d'arbres."

"Voici une église," he was just starting to say when he noticed with dread the sign pointing the wrong way. His heart drummed as he hit the turn signal and pulled over under a cluster of trees where the truck couldn't be seen from the road.

Stepping down from the safety of the Ranger into the leaves, Martin whispered, "Je ne veux pas mourir," before shuffling into the woods.

The nights were cooling off with the end of summer, but the breeze was still warm, and floating on it, Martin could make out an aroma more human and not strictly of woods. As he moved further through the leaves, the smell began to take shape, seemingly changing the temperature of the forest, and grew still warmer and more pungent, rich and oily and slightly sour, as Martin walked on, holding his hands out before him to fend off stray twigs.

"Cette odeur est atroce," he murmured to himself, unable to contain it. Just as he did, the unmistakable smell of cigarette smoke overtook the sweetness of the air and the click of metal split the darkness.

"Ne me tuez pas," Martin pleaded.

He stood frozen and an impatient voice from behind the gun said, "What?"

"Please don't kill me," he said.

"You're French."

Martin scrambled for the right answer.

"You speak French?" the voice said louder; it would not ask again.

Martin knew that admitting to speaking French was never a good idea, but lying seemed a bigger mistake, so he said, "Oui."

"What do you need?" the voice asked after a smoky pause.

Martin forced out, "Un gun."

There was another long pause.

"Colonel doesn't usually like visitors during table tennis, but..."

The man led Martin deeper into the woods, where the smell covered him like a hot blanket. His eyes watered, blurring the little he could see in the solid darkness, but the path beneath his feet felt well-worn. He clenched his fists and resolved not to mention the smell, though it was impossible to imagine how the man with the gun was enduring it.

When they reached a clearing in the woods, Martin rubbed his eyes and tried to get a look around.

A series of shacks were laid out before them like a small industrial town. The man led Martin up to one of the bigger buildings and stuck his head in the door, nodding to someone inside. He held the door open for Martin to walk through.

"Wait here," he grumbled as he passed through another door, leaving Martin in the chipboard vestibule.

The man returned a moment later and, without looking Martin in the eye, asked him to conjugate the subjunctive of the verb *to love* in French. Martin couldn't believe it. The subjunctive had been one of the hardest tenses to learn and though he still never knew when to use it, he employed the trick he had learned for remembering it by mentally inserting *it is imperative that* before the verb. *It is imperative that I love. It is imperative that you love*...And so, mechanically, he rhymed it off. Then the man showed him a picture of a hat, hastily rendered on a sheet of notebook paper, and asked him what it was. He knew, perhaps better than anything, that the picture was not of a hat, but of a snake digesting an elephant, and shouted that out like a game-show contestant. The man held the drawing straight out and looked at it, then disappeared again behind the door.

Martin hadn't expected this kind of test. These were questions he not only knew the answers to, but was dying to be asked.

The door opened again from the inside, and the impatient voice said, "Mon."

The room was made of the same particle board as the entranceway, but with huge swaths of purple velvet haphazardly tacked on the walls. Two men sat on a worn gold sofa, each with a long beard cut off at a blunt angle and a pit-bull terrier at his feet. In one corner of the room stood a bar covered in brown Naugahyde, with several open bottles of wine and a few half-full glasses atop it. A Ping-Pong game was underway on a table in the middle of the room. Another bearded man had just served to a man in an ivory cable-knit sweater. As the latter followed through on the missed serve, he turned his face toward Martin, who stifled a gasp.

"Aie! Bonjour," the man said, placing his paddle down on the table. The man approached him, hand extended, and said, "Je suis le Colonel Ouide."

There was something strange about the Colonel's French, but it was hard for Martin to put his finger on it with all that was going on with the Colonel's face. Martin wiped his hand on his pant leg before returning the unexpected handshake, trying to think of his own name.

"Je m'appelle Martin Bureau," he found the presence of mind to say. He had to concentrate to figure out how the parts of the Colonel's face worked together: the oily brown curls, the thick bottom lip, the bulbous nose. Without question, his face was unusual, but it was only as Martin's eyes travelled outward that he got the full impact of the ears. From behind each of the Colonel's cowlicky sideburns protruded an ear the size of an English muffin. He couldn't look away.

"Où avez-vous appris votre français?" the Colonel asked.

France! The Colonel was from France. He didn't know how he knew, but Martin knew. He felt giddy.

"Je lis des livres et j'écoute des cassettes et j'aime beaucoup le français," said Martin.

"*Le Petit Prince* est le meilleur histoire au monde," said the Colonel.

"C'est mon livre favori," said Martin eagerly, committing an unpardonable anglicism.

The Colonel languorously lit a cigarette, inhaled deeply, and let his head roll back as he exhaled.

"Dis-moi, what is your favourite part of these buke?"

Martin wished he didn't speak French so badly that the Colonel felt he needed to speak English badly.

Books were hard to come by in Pinto, even at the bookstore, but when he'd started learning French, Martin had found a copy of *Le Petit Prince* in a bin outside Readies' Books and had read it easily a hundred times. He knew the answer to this question, too, though it no longer felt like a test. The fox. The fox was the reason he would turn the book over and start reading again from the beginning. Each time the story ended, he missed the fox.

Martin stared and stared at the Colonel's ears and said, "Le renard," in case there was a chance they could speak French again.

Colonel Weed exhaled toward the ceiling and said softly, "Le renard..."

He nodded approvingly, his thoughts visibly elsewhere. Martin shifted his weight from one foot to the other. He could feel a moustache of perspiration.

"Le renard, he's very important. To learn to make a friend."

Tentatively, Martin said, "Quel est votre favourite part?"

The Colonel turned his strange face upward and said, "La rose, bien sûr."

Martin nodded enthusiastically, though he had never understood why the prince was so keen on it. The rose was vain and dishonest, while the fox was calm and profound and genuinely cared about the prince. Nevertheless, the Colonel clearly had a stake in the rose and Martin wasn't about to mention his misgivings.

"Jean-Claude," said the Colonel, directing his voice behind him. "Du fromage."

The impatient man from outside ducked behind the curtain and the Colonel beckoned Martin to follow him to the Naugahyde bar. He poured two short glasses of wine and passed one to Martin.

"Le Prince," said the Colonel, lifting his glass.

"Le Prince," said Martin.

The Colonel took a contemplative swig, dramatically permitting the wine to rest on his tongue for a moment before swallowing. Martin reproduced the Colonel's exact motions and satisfied reaction. The taste was complex and fruity, dark and mysterious. He had never understood the swishing and all the ceremony of wine, but this tasted different than any other wine he'd had. He had never wanted so badly to keep something resting on his tongue. It seemed a shame to swallow it.

"C'est mon Gamay Noir," said the Colonel.

Martin nodded, though the words meant nothing.

Jean Claude returned from the backroom with a plate of cheese, which he placed in front of Martin. Here, beyond any doubt, was the source of the smell that permeated the forest.

"Je le fabrique myself," the Colonel said.

Martin took a gulp of air, then timidly picked up a lump and put it in his mouth, unsure what to do once it got there. He brought his palate down to crush it and found that the smell had no bearing on the taste. In fact, its foul smell was exactly matched by its deliciousness. He had never tasted such cheese. No one else ate, and the Colonel's eyes remained on Martin's face as he devoured every crumb.

The moment the plate was clean, Jean-Claude swept in to remove it. He returned a moment later with a big leather case, which he gently set down on the bar before the Colonel.

The Colonel adjusted the high neck of his sweater and opened the case. "Et bien, mon ami?"

Martin had forgotten why he was there, and when he cast his eyes over the row of firearms, he nearly screamed.

The Colonel said softly, "And for what, you? What will you do with this gun?" He looked Martin straight in the eye as he spoke.

"It isn't for me," Martin said. "It's for a friend."

"You are here, very afraid, buying a gun for a friend," the Colonel said, more testing out the words than requesting confirmation.

"I want to do him a favour," said Martin.

The Colonel looked at him for a long time. "You have such a friend, that for him you would do such a favour?"

Martin contemplated telling him Réjean's situation, but instead said, "He's my best friend. I'd do anything for him."

The Colonel searched Martin's face curiously, his eyes flickering back and forth, then reached behind him into the waistband of his pants and pulled out a gun. Martin jumped back.

"It is correct," said the Colonel, turning the handle of the gun to face Martin and laying it flat in his palm. "Voici."

"God, that really scared me," Martin said.

The Colonel laughed. So did the bearded men on the couch.

Martin slowly reached for the gun. It was compact and beautiful and terrifying.

"These one is mine," the Colonel said. "Un Glock G9. Comme la police."

Martin wrapped his damp hand around the gun in the only way he could imagine holding one. It was incredibly light. He placed his finger on the trigger and felt an uncanny shift in the atmosphere of the room. He pointed it at the floor. Holding it in his hand made him think differently about the word *handgun*.

"How much?" he asked.

"Take-le," said the Colonel quietly with a nod. "Your friend, he's lucky to know a man like you."

Martin shook his head.

"Garde," said the Colonel. "Men who come to see me, they are all the same. They are closed. They are closed up. In their face you can see there is no way in. All around me are these men." He turned and gestured toward the men on the couch. "These ones, they work for me, but do we understand each other? Do they make a joke to me? I know them now many years, and do they ever make a joke on my ears? Non. Look at them, my ears!"

"They're huge," said Martin, at last.

The Colonel smiled, nodding his head with satisfaction. "Oui. Ils sont énormes." He spent a moment in quiet appreciation of Martin, sizing him up. "Take this and give it to your friend. He must know how he is lucky."

Martin managed to nod solemnly and put the gun in his pocket. They sipped their wine and Martin thanked Réjean in his heart for having taught him to drink in silence.

NOW

Agathe stood at the bus stop, lighting a cigarette with her shoulders to the wind, when the crunch of tires on gravel advanced on her suddenly. She spun around and pitched her lighter at the car in a split-second defensive move, and it bounced off the windshield of the Civic.

Debbie rolled down the window and blew out smoke. "Jesus, do you always throw things at people trying to help you?" she said. "Get in!"

Agathe grabbed her lighter and hurried to the passenger side, pausing for a moment as she lifted her foot from the cold morning roadside into the smoky pod of noise with its already familiar fragrance of Player's Light, coconut suntan lotion, and Love's Baby Soft.

"You live all the way out here?" said Debbie, peeling away from the shoulder. "Jesus. I'll pick you up. You can't be taking that bus. Don't be crazy. You wanna smoke?"

"J'en ai," said Agathe. She lit one and sank back into the leatherette.

The radio was playing a song about a barracuda.

"I hope you don't mind the radio. I need to rock out to get myself right in the morning," yelled Debbie, turning it up.

Dun-duhduh-dun-duhduh-dun-duhduh-dun-duhduh-dun-duhduh-dun-duhduh-dun-duhduhdundun. WEEEEE EEEEEEEEEEEEEEEEEEEEEEEEEEEEEEEEEEEEEEEEE EEEEEEEEEEW!

It sounded just like a barracuda might, if it made noise.

Réjean's music didn't do this. It didn't sound like it was chasing you through the water.

Dun-duhduh-dun-duhduh-dun-duhduh-dun-duh-duh-dun-duhduh-dun-duhduh-dun-duhduhdundun. WEEEEEEEEEEEEEEEEEWEEEEEEEWEEEEEEEE-EEEEEEEEEEEEEEW!

"Do you like Heart?" yelled Debbie.

"Oui!" yelled Agathe.

"Nancy Wilson is amazing. Listen to her, she's like a jack-hammer!"

Agathe felt loose but alert as she watched the woodland passing. This was what it sounded like in those trees, with Nancy Wilson, jackhammering. It was like she was controlling the radio, or like she *was* the radio. Debbie pounded her flat palm against the roof, and Agathe laughed, her eyes like two walnuts.

"Hey, are you married?" yelled Debbie.

Agathe considered lying, but decided not to. "Mon mari..." she yelled after a brief hesitation, then paused again long enough that Debbie looked over and turned down Heart. "Mon mari, Réjean, y...y left me," she said, thinking it was about time to admit the truth.

"What?" said Debbie. "How stupid was he?"

Agathe looked at the dirty pants protector under her feet. "Ben, c'est compliqué."

"How long were you married?"

"Vingt ans."

"And he just picked up and left?"

"Ben..." said Agathe, "c'est compliqué."

She dug out her wallet and held it open to the picture of the two of them on their wedding day.

"Jesus Christ," said Debbie, swerving out of the lane, then

back into it, her neck bent to Agathe's wallet. "Look at him!"

Debbie was no longer watching the road.

"Wow," she said, "I don't mean to rub it in, but...wow." She reached for the wallet and held it in front of her on the steering wheel. "He's massive," she said, and looked up at Agathe. "No, I'm sorry, I'm not even gonna ask. It's vulgar..."

"C'était énorme," Agathe wistfully assured her.

Debbie nodded appreciatively, still looking at the picture. "I've never been married," she said, handing the wallet back. "I've only fallen in love once and never again. Not since Dale."

"Ah oui?"

"We met when we were nineteen, and were together for like five years. I don't know if you want to hear this right now."

"Ben sûr," said Agathe.

"Well, it was perfect. It was a perfect love. We were like the same person. We even had the same hair. Dale would try on my clothes and put on my makeup, and I can't even tell you how much fun that was. Dale was the one who told me I should try out for the Valkyries. He said I was the best dancer he'd ever seen. And I went to every one of Roxxx-lyde's shows—that was his band—and screamed my head off. We both really wanted each other to succeed."

Success for Dale was self-evident, consisting only of rock-and-roll stardom, while Debbie imagined herself standing at a podium in a gown, accepting an award—she just hadn't yet decided what for.

"Et alors?" said Agathe.

"Well," said Debbie, "this is going to sound weird, but...I had to break up with him because of Peter Frampton. This producer came to see the guys play at an all-ages club and signed them that night. From the second they signed that contract, Dale was famous. It was so fast. You don't real-ize how fast it can be when there's someone there, ready to make money off you. He was setting up a tour for them—like, to the States—and that's when I was like, okay, there were gonna be a lot of girls falling in love with Dale, throwing their panties...Dale was hot. A guy like that just can't have an old lady. I knew that. When I was listening to *Frampton Comes Alive!* lying on the floor of my bedroom, no one even had to tell me that Peter Frampton had a wife. I just knew. I knew that he wrote all those songs for her, not me, and it sort of ruined the experience, to be honest. For me and for Peter. I mean, I'll always love Frampton, and that album, but I really felt—*I really felt*—that Dale deserved to have all those girls feel the way I felt about Frampton. I didn't want to deprive him of that. But it was mostly, honestly, for those girls. They had every right to believe that he could love them back. I mean, it's rock and roll." Debbie crushed out her cigarette in the ashtray. "So I let him go."

"Ouaou..." said Agathe.

"Now he does community theatre," Debbie said. "Not that there's anything wrong with that. He's got a wife and two kids and they live in the suburbs, and I do my thing."

Debbie's thing was a gentle "Aw, hon, that's okay," for any man who showed interest. The guy would come away feeling apologetic, grateful, and unsure of whether or not he'd just tried to ask her out. It was a good trick.

Agathe could only shake her head. "Let 'im go..." she said.

They drove in silence for a time.

"Was it sort of a relief?" asked Debbie.

"Comment?"

"I mean, I could see it being a relief, when your husband left. Because you'd be free. Some people find it a drag to have someone around all the time..."

"Non," said Agathe. "Non, it wasn't." She was finished talking about Réjean. "Hoos this?" she asked, turning up the radio on a sly, purring voice telling them to bang a gong.

"Oh," said Debbie. "Oh, now *this*—" she lit another cigarette—"this is T-Rex." She lifted her chin heavenward, as though T-Rex was in the sky. "Just listen." They listened. "And *that* is Marc Bolan. Have you ever heard anything so perfect?" Debbie dipped her head reverently, and said with a kind of wonder, "Did you know that Marc Bolan was so tiny you could fit him in a dollhouse?"

She told Agathe about the children of the Beltane Wood and Marc Bolan's amazing jumpsuits all the way to Dingwall's Donuts.

"His death was the greatest tragedy in the history of...in history," she said, pulling up to the drive-thru speaker, "but it doesn't mean he and I can't still be in love. And I happen to know for a fact he can still feel my love, all the way from the forest of Beltane."

In addition to needing the radio to get her started in the morning, Debbie also needed a large tea from Dingwall's, with cream, bag in—just as Agathe took hers. This became a ritual that Agathe would begin to look forward to, much in the way she suspected Debbie looked forward to loudly saying the words *bag in* into the drive-thru speaker. As they waited to drive up to the pickup window, Debbie turned up the radio and said, "Aw, listen to Bruce."

A guitar came together with a drum and what sounded like one of every other instrument, each playing one note

83

or hitting one beat, together, in an important cascade as it walked down a staircase to a cliff-hanging smash that resonated for just long enough that it didn't seem to have anything left. Then: two-three-four.

The highway was jammed with broken heroes on a last-chance power drive, everyone was out on the run, and there was nowhere left to hide. Bruce's voice bled with abandon, like he had tried everything and couldn't think of a better plan.

"He's so frustrated," said Debbie. "He wants something new and he doesn't know what, he just knows it's out there somewhere and he needs to get Wendy and get out of that town before it crushes them both. Listen to him. No one understands desperation like Bruce. And no one under-stands hope like Bruce. And he's got my favourite ass."

She passed over Agathe's tea and pulled them into a parking spot to listen to the rest of the song. Debbie closed her eyes and raised her fist, singing along with Bruce about walking in the sun. Agathe closed her eyes, too, and nodded along. When the song was almost over, she peeped through one eye at Debbie, who still had both of hers closed.

When she opened them, she said, "Hey, why don't you drive? You don't have a car?"

"Ah," said Agathe, "Ché pas comment."

"You never learned?"

"Non, c'était Réjean qui faisait le driving."

Debbie pulled out of the drive-thru and into the adjoin-ing pharmacy's empty parking lot. She took off her seat belt. "Get behind the wheel. You need to know how. You can't just not know how."

Juste comme ça. No one had ever offered to show her. But she had watched Réjean go through the driving motions like a dance so many times she almost knew how.

Debbie took her through the positions of the gearshift.

"Now you have to be firm, but gentle," said Debbie, making a stroking gesture on the handle of the stick. "The knob is the most important part," she said, further caressing it. After a few more jerking and stroking motions to make her point, she went through the gears.

"Okay, so these are the positions: first, second, third, fourth, fifth, and reverse. Remember, the clutch lets you change them; when you forget the clutch, you grind the gears. I always find it funny when people say that, 'Y'know what grinds my gears?' Anyway, now you'll know why they say that. Because it's so irritating. And it's bad for the car."

Agathe mentally shifted through the gears, her head following their pattern.

"Okay, now press the clutch, and pull the stick from neutral to the one position."

Agathe did, and the Civic started to move forward. She brought her foot down on the gas, ready to make it go faster, grinding the gears.

"Ooooooooooh, you wanna go fast, eh?" said Debbie.

After a few more jerky tries, and practising the fineries of releasing the clutch, Agathe did a circle of the empty lot, hand over hand. Debbie, banging her palm on the ceiling, bellowed, "Yes! YEEEEEEEEEEEEES!! Now stroke the knob, and shift up! SHIFT UP!!"

She must have been a terrific cheerleader.

From then on, Debbie insisted that Agathe drive in the mornings, both because she needed to learn and because Debbie loved being chauffeured. She would shout encouragement from the passenger seat as she put on her makeup in the visor mirror.

"You were born to drive. Lookit you!"

Agathe couldn't believe she'd ever let someone else do all the driving. Réjean made so much more sense now. She understood how much of his general happiness came from operating a vehicle. What surprised her, once she'd broken the 110- kilometre speed limit on the highway, was Réjean's ability to maintain a reasonable speed. He'd always been such a cautious driver, whereas Agathe got impatient when she and Debbie would hit a red light, and was disappointed every time they reached their destination. She got a chill of excitement whenever a transport truck flew by. Those trucks gave her a feeling, way up there. Like they ran things.

Agathe and Debbie stood on the loading dock on a Friday afternoon, smoking a second cigarette.

"Any plans for the weekend?" asked Debbie.

Agathe snorted and shook her head. "Non."

"Do you do anything for fun? Jesus!"

Agathe felt she could tell Debbie anything, but still knew better than to mention Sondage.

"Okay. Tonight, we go out. Rip this town a new one."

Agathe rode on anticipation for the rest of the day, occasionally stealing excited glances at Debbie.

Between repairing and selling merchandise, Debbie was the best business plan Stereoblast had ever had. Whereas Tony, when the store wasn't busy, performed cleaning tasks like grouping things in threes, Debbie was productive nearly all the time, and had increased revenue by thirty-eight percent. She had outsold herself that afternoon, and when Wood locked the door after the last customer, he turned to her and said, "Lookit. Tony and me, Tony and I are gonna...y'know...celebrate. Can we...beer?

"Aw, hon, that's okay," said Debbie with a deep tilt of her head.

Wood apologized, and Tony led him out the front doors.

Debbie turned to Agathe, shook her hair, gave a loud "WOOOO!" and threw her purse over her shoulder. "C'mon," Debbie barked. "Let's go get loaded!"

In the Civic, the radio played a song about a lady with the night in her veins.

"Ooh," said Debbie, and turned it up, "This is the Pretenders. This one's dirty, you'll like this. That's Chrissie Hynde. Listen to her."

Agathe brought her face closer to the steering wheel as she watched the beautiful road.

"So she's super horny, and when she's talking about the night being inside her, what she really means is that this guy is inside her—or maybe she really is talking about the night. Anyway, it's super hot. Here, he's got his chest on her back cross a new Cadillac. Like, what a dirty thing to say. It's so dirty."

They listened to Chrissie Hynde and her dirty song.

"Chrissie can do anything she wants," Debbie yelled. "She plays guitar *and* sings *and* plays the harmonica, and has these amazing bangs. She just holds the whole thing together—listen to her. The rest of the Pretenders are guys too—*helping* her sing this song about screwing this guy. God..."

In the crowded parking lot at the Whisky Mak, Debbie fluffed up her hair and reached down the neckline of her sweater into each armpit to pull up a handful of speckled bosom. Agathe tugged her track suit top down over her midsection and stood with her hands on her hips, watching as

Debbie applied lip gloss, punctuating with a pouty smack. When Debbie flung open the red doors of the Whisky Mak, it was as though revealing herself at last to a crowd that had bought tickets to see her.

The sudden blare of the music hit Agathe like a wave. They had been listening to rock and roll at work and in the car since Debbie started, but never at this volume, filling a room this size, getting into every pore. It filled her up in a way that awakened all her nerves and made her stand taller. Rock and roll had a way of putting itself on you, so that you were wearing whatever was being sung. All the abandon and rage and torment and heartache. Everyone here was wearing it. Réjean's music didn't do this.

A sharp pain jabbed her heart as she thought of those sweet Acadian songs. One hundred and ninety-eight days he'd been gone, and nothing Agathe could do would bring him back.

She forced her eyes open and turned her attention to the Thin Lizzie song now playing. She and Debbie had talked about this one, and she liked the feeling of menace about it, that the boys were coming back into town and if they wanted to fight, you'd better let 'em. The song put itself on Agathe, and she became part of the menace. Réjean's face slipped from her thoughts.

Debbie turned with a flip of her hair and said, "This is Thin Lizzie."

"Hi know!" yelled Agathe.

Debbie beckoned her up to the bar, where she shouted that they would get faster service. There were two empty stools there, one of which was being leaned against by a thick young man in a long black coat and glasses. Debbie turned back to Agathe and poked her chin into the air.

She nudged her breasts between the young man and his skinny companion.

"You boys saving this seat for anyone special?"

"No, I was just leaning on that stool. It's not officially occupied. You may sit on it."

"Well, thank you," said Debbie. "Looks like someone's momma raised him right. Whaddya have, Agathe?" Debbie asked, turning her head partway around.

Agathe shrugged. "Ché pas, là."

A moment later, two brown bottles of Alpine were deposited on the counter in front of Debbie, who passed one to Agathe. They clinked them together and each took a long swig.

"So this is Agathe. We work at the Stereoblast over at Convenience Place. Whaddyou guys do? Fix computers or what?"

"Actually, we create the programs that run the computers. We're programmers."

Debbie turned to Agathe. "I'm sorry, I have to do some networking here."

Agathe took another swig of beer, then another. She wasn't interested in talking to the computer guys. She had never used a computer. More importantly, she had never sat in a bar where rock and roll changed her physical being. She let the music envelop her again and took a long look around. People shouted at each other, bringing mouths to ears and ears to mouths. There were other women there dressed like Debbie. There were men together, looking at women and women together, looking at men. Two women caught Agathe's eye. They sat on the opposite side of the U-shaped bar, a few seats down from each other. One woman wore a purple sweater with a fur collar and looked straight ahead as though listening politely to someone who wasn't there. The other woman wore a professional blouse, like a secretary. She was reading a book, occasionally writing in the margins, smoking. From time to time, she would close her book and take a long sip of an amber-coloured drink. Agathe wondered whether the two women knew each other.

She turned away from Debbie and the computer guys and pretended she was one of these women, like the three of them were members of a club. She took a few more sips of her beer, trying to look nonchalant.

Off to the side of the bar was an empty dance floor, though a semicircle of women danced just next to it. At the back of the bar, in a sort of alcove, was an area that looked to be intended for custodial use—Agathe instinctively identified the mop leaning against the wall by the self-wringing handle. The alcove also contained a pool table and a cigarette machine, and a few scattered tables. In the far corner a man sat alone at one of them. His attire looked vaguely industrial. Agathe had almost scanned past him when her stomach leaped into her throat. His clothes weren't industrial, they were military. He was drinking from a brown bottle, singing, and nodding his head with the momentum of the song. He really approved of this song. There wasn't much to do with this one, except agree.

Something about him was so unreal. It was hard to imagine him speaking or eating, doing things normal people do. Stranger still was that no one else seemed to notice him. Even though he was singing—even though he was singing passionately—he didn't seem to want anyone's attention. It was just for him.

Agathe shrank back behind Debbie's hair and spied on

him as a tinkling electronic keyboard started up the next song. Agathe sighed. The slow ones took forever, and were all about love, which she tried not to think about. In this one, someone had never needed love like he needed her.

Debbie turned from her networking to Agathe. "This is Sheriff," she said. "They're Canadian!"

Agathe shook a cigarette from her pack and lit it as couples started vacating the back tables for the dance floor, leaving the army man starkly conspicuous and easy to watch past Debbie's hair. When the song came to the chorus, the man opened his eyes, raised a gentle fist and sang, long and heartfelt, "BAY-bay-eeyay-eeyayay, oo I get chills when I'm with you, owhoa whoa, owhoa whoa."

It was a perfect Baby: loud and explosive and precisely the way it was supposed to sound. Of course the army man understood Baby. Of course he did. Baby was one of Agathe's favourite parts of rock and roll. It was a word she almost never used, except when Réjean was being one. Baby was what you called the person you fought to love. It had a tragic, sexy overtone: Baby please don't go. Baby Imma want you. Baby come back. Baby made you do crazy things. You had to earn Baby with a certain amount of abandon that she now wondered if she and Réjean had ever had.

The man was just reaching the end of the last oooooo of the chorus when she saw him squint at her past Debbie's hair. The man quickly closed his eyes and began to sing the next verse, which he did with even more conviction than the first one. When the next chorus came, he turned his body toward her, drummed the air, pointed, and sang straight to her, "BAY-bay-eeyay-eeyayay oo I get chills when I'm with you, owhoa whoa, owhoa whoa."

It was too much. Agathe finally laughed and the man grinned and turned slightly away from her and drummed the air for the next Baby.

When he came to the final falsetto—when I'm with youuuuuuuuu, ooo, OO—he turned and delivered it straight to her. She laughed again, but with the end of the song, wasn't sure what to do next. A harder song started up, devouring the last tender strains.

Dun dudda dun dudda dun dudda dun dudda dun dudda dun dudda dun...

Sonofabitch, thought Agathe, relieved.

This one was about Nazareth taking a flight they shouldn't have gotten on, and was written by Joni Mitchell, whom Debbie said was a Holy Entity. The man must like this one, too. Agathe peeked past Debbie again, but where the army man had been, there was only an empty bottle.

"Hey! Crazy Yellow Guy! No way!" Debbie shouted.

Agathe turned to watch the crazy guy in the yellow raincoat from the mall head out the door. The army man was nowhere in sight.

THEN

Saturday morning, Réjean had been staring at the ceiling, amending his fishing lie since two a.m., when the rain started. Now it was getting light out and there was no break in the downpour.

He hadn't heard back from Martin about the gun. It had only been a day, but he didn't feel he could leave it any longer. He'd realized the foolishness of the request as soon as the words left his mouth. Smart guys like Martin didn't do things like buy guns. He almost wished he hadn't asked, but couldn't help it; whenever he needed advice these days, he found himself taking the turnoff for the Chevy dealership. He wished he had told Martin about his hobby earlier. Perhaps Martin could have offered him some guidance, but it was too late now for advice. For the first time in his life, Réjean felt fear. He could barely function at work, and nearly walked away from a falling tree before the panicked shouts of the team brought him back. He had been sleeping with one eye open since the Lobster Shack parking lot. Gun or no gun, he needed to find the man and let him know that if he came near Agathe again, he would be killed.

Réjean turned to look at Agathe, gently snoring, and tried to remember the time before he had ever told her a lie. She had been unexpectedly happy when he told her the men from work had invited him to go fishing. While it was a terrible lie, he had run through the feasibility of it in his head and come up with enough justification to make it work. The main problems, namely his disinterest in fishing and the onset of autumn, could be explained away as the catalysts for the invitation: Réjean had never gone fishing with them and the season was almost over. This would be their last chance that year, and they had insisted.

From what Réjean understood about fishing, it took a long time. Long enough for him to find the man and do whatever needed to be done. He might need to hurt him, and the idea made him physically sick.

As he watched Agathe sleep, he reminded himself to show only negligible disappointment and tell her that people fished in the rain all the time, that the fish would be more plentiful, because they came out in greater numbers when it rained, figuring all the fishermen would be at home.

When it rained on a workday for Réjean, he and the guys on the crew would pack up and head back to the mill, where they would drink coffee and play Forty-Fives. On those days, Agathe would send Réjean to work with a dozen of her date squares. Often, as they made love on the kitchen floor, he would describe to her just what an animal frenzy her date squares aroused in the guys from work.

"Tes carrés de dates…" he would murmur in her ear.

Réjean brushed the hair from Agathe's eyes and, still asleep, she blindly swatted his hand and covered her face.

Over breakfast, he found it hard to stick to his intentions and caught himself sighing, then trying to cover by upwardly inflecting it into a happy sigh, the kind you might hear from someone who was looking forward to going fishing.

As she prepared his sandwiches, Agathe eyed him. He eyed her back from beneath his brows as he picked up crumbs, one by one, from the table with his finger.

She stopped and turned. "Aie, ça va, mon amour?"

He rose from the table and wrapped his arms around her where she stood with a butter knife in one hand and the lid of the mustard in the other. "Oui, oui," he said. "Tu vas me manquer, c'est tout," and he held her tighter, enveloping her completely, miserable.

As he guided the Silverado cautiously through the pouring rain, Réjean glanced down at his hands on the wheel and tried to picture the impact of his fist against the army man's face. He winced and tried to envision another scene, one where they calmly discussed the situation and reached a compromise, but when he thought back on the man shouting at Agathe from the window of his truck, that seemed unlikely.

The first part of the plan was clear enough: find the F-100. He peered through the windshield at every vehicle on the road, looking for dirty brown trucks. He would check back at the places he'd previously seen the man, and other places in town, like Convenience Place Mall, but he would also check places that an army man might spend time, like the racetrack or the hospital. If all else failed, there was a military base two townships over, although the idea of surrounding himself with other army men didn't seem like a smart thing to do. Réjean concentrated and imagined the next step. Once he had found the truck, he would have to approach the man and say something like "Scusez" or "Monsieur, un moment." Or perhaps a plain "Hé." Or maybe he'd just grab him by the collar, pin him against the side of his truck, and get straight to threatening him. If Réjean caught him by surprise, the man may not have time to remember he wasn't afraid.

The perfect outcome would be to avoid a physical altercation entirely. They would talk. What if Réjean apologized for writing *LAVE-MOI* on the man's truck? What if he apologized profusely? "Je me confounds en excuses," he would say. He already felt legitimate regret at having hurt the man's feelings, so he wouldn't even be pretending. He could say something even more contrite, like, "Chus tellement sorry, là. J'aurais pas dû écrire sur votre truck. C'était pas nice, ça." Everyone loved an apology. He tried to picture a softening in the man's face with the appreciation that Réjean had sought him out, a stranger, all the way across town, just to apologize. Then the man would leave Agathe alone.

He looked down again at his hands on the wheel, still free from brutality. Kind hands. Loving, useful hands. And as he struggled with images of what he might have to do with them, his wedding ring caught his eye and he nearly drove off the road.

Their anniversary.

White-knuckled, he stared into the oncoming sheets of rain.

It was next week. He had to make something for her. He'd completely forgotten, with his hobby taking up all his time.

Normally, he would take the exit just off the old road and feel the calm wash over him as the big blue sign with the golden Chevrolet crest loomed into view, but Réjean felt too ashamed to go back and ask Martin's advice again. The only thing to do was drive, and think, and look for the Ford. As he was doing all those things, he spotted a set of headlights stopped at the side of the road. Coming closer, he identified the vehicle as a Ford, but not an F-100; this one was new and blue, its hood open with a plume of smoke rising from within. Réjean hesitated, but could not ignore a distressed vehicle, Ford or not.

When Martin got home from the Colonel's, tingling with disbelief, he sat down at the kitchen table with the gun. He couldn't stop looking at it. It was truly beautiful. He turned it this way and that on his autumn-scene placemat. He picked it up, aimed it at the refrigerator, and said, "Attention."

He put it down. He picked it up again, impressed every time. It didn't have a six-chamber holder like the cowboy guns he'd seen on TV. Instead, it had a magazine, which was easier to manage than he would have thought. You clicked it out, you clicked it back in. He took a bath with the gun on the side of the tub, and slept with it on his night table, reaching for it from time to time to make sure it was still there. But his fondness for the gun in no way outweighed his excitement at the thought of presenting it to Réjean. He would call him first thing when he got to work on Monday. He had never called him on the telephone, though he had his number on file. He would say something like "I got it," and listen for the relief in Réjean's voice as he said, "Merci, Martin."

Saturday morning, he awoke to the sound of a downpour. The success of his trip to Colonel Weed's had lifted his spirits and with the rain that now beckoned and with the promise of sloppy ground, he could think of only one way to spend this day: off-roading.

Because he couldn't bear to leave it at home, he brought the gun along. As he donned his rain gear, the temporary owner of an implement of menace, he saw a knight shielded by an impenetrable suit of yellow armour, a waterproof crusader. Imperméable.

In the Ranger, the windshield wipers splatted back and forth, only momentarily clearing the spot of windshield in front of his eyes before closing up again into a sheet of pure water. He looked down at the gun on the passenger seat and smiled. He wondered if, when he presented it to Réjean, perhaps Réjean would pat him on the shoulder or better yet, slap him on the arm.

He had nearly reached his destination when the Ranger began to lose power. It stopped responding to his foot on the accelerator and through the rain he saw a puff of smoke rise from the hood. With his remaining momentum, he pulled over to the shoulder.

The Ranger had never given him a moment's trouble, and he was confounded as to what could be wrong. Despite his familiarity with the features, options, and fuel consumption of trucks, he knew nothing about fixing one. He had never even changed a tire. He had, however, opened up the hoods of countless vehicles to display shiny new engines to poten-tial buyers and knew that when your truck broke down, you checked the engine. He pulled the release latch under the dashboard and stepped down into the mud. Without any idea what to look for, he stuck his head under the open hood.

Through the hissing of the obstinate engine, he heard the crunch of tires on the gravel as another vehicle pulled up behind the Ranger. Holding his sou'wester on his head against the onslaught of rain, he ducked out and was morti-fied to see a shiny black Silverado looming like a mountain.

Réjean sprang from the truck and jogged toward the Ranger. Martin pulled down the rim of his sou'wester, but quickly reminded himself that only a chicken would try to hide beneath a hat. Feeling melodramatic, he squared off with Réjean and raised his chin to face him.

As he took in Martin, at first Réjean's face lit up. But then he glanced at the Ranger, then back to Martin, then to the truck again. He slowed up, stopping dead a few feet from him, his face clouded with confusion.

At a loss, Martin said, "I don't know what's wrong with it."

Réjean stood anchored to the spot, then shook his head, nodded, walked haltingly past Martin, and stuck his head beneath the hood. As Réjean stooped over the engine, Martin read a hundred things in his back, most notably, he was sure, that their friendship was over. Réjean poked around for a moment and re-emerged promptly.

"Ce n'est que le battery," he shouted economically over the rain. "Je vais te donner un jump."

As Réjean turned and headed back to the Silverado, he glanced again at the Ranger, then back at Martin, the rain dripping off the tip of his unprotected nose, and Martin remembered the gun still sitting in plain view on the passenger seat. He wondered if Réjean would even accept his gift now that he knew about Martin's disloyalty to the Chevy brand.

Réjean climbed back into the Silverado and drove it down the slippery shoulder and around to the front of the Ranger so his jumper cables could reach the battery. Martin came around to where Réjean stood between the two trucks and watched ineffectually. Not only had he been caught in a lie and now felt like a sneaky fool, but he also felt overdressed and incompetent as Réjean got soaked performing a task that every man but Martin was sure instinctively to know how to do.

Réjean attached the cable clamps to his own battery and started the engine.

"Bon," he shouted over the rain. "Try-le."

Martin bowed his head and walked around to the driver side. As he climbed in, he reached over and quickly swept the gun off the seat onto the floor, where it sat conspicuously as Réjean walked around to the driver side to supervise.

Martin turned the key in the ignition and the engine made a coughing sound. He tried again and got the same thing.

"Laisse-moi," Réjean said.

Martin hesitated for too long. He wanted so badly to say something but he couldn't put the words together. This was not the way it was meant to go.

"Beunh, voyons," said Réjean, rain cascading down his face.

Martin stepped down from the truck and looked weakly at Réjean as they traded spots. As Réjean set his boot in the door, his eyes went straight to the black object on the passenger-side floor. He lifted the rest of himself into the cab, adjusting the seat so he could fit, still gazing down. He glanced at Martin on the rainy shoulder and cocked his head just barely.

Martin stared down at the ground.

Réjean took hold of the keys and positioned his foot on the gas in preparation for the delicate jig of pedals. The engine started to cough, then turned over, then began to purr regularly. Réjean climbed down from the truck, and Martin watched him disconnect the jumper cables, returning them to a box in the Silverado's cab. When Réjean released the hood of the Silverado and dusted off his now greasy hands, Martin said, "Wait."

He reached into the Ranger, plucked the gun from the floor and said, "It's for you. The gun. You asked if I could find you one and I went out and found you one. I did that for you."

Réjean looked from the gun to Martin to the Ford Ranger rumbling next to them. Martin dropped his gaze from Réjean's unreadable face. Réjean finally lifted his hand and wiped the rain from his moustache. "C'nest pas un crime, Martin," he laughed, "driver un Ford."

And as if in a dream, he reached out a soaking hand and

slapped Martin's yellow arm. Everything was fine. He was kidding. Kidding. Of course. It was what guys did. It was all Martin had ever wanted, all his life, so when it happened he didn't know enough to see it. He was sure that with more practice he could get it right. He desperately wished he had brought along some rum. They could have one right here on the roadside. He wanted to start over with Réjean, without the omissions and untruths.

Réjean shook his head as raindrops flew from the tips of his hair, and Martin sensed the full ridiculousness of such a secret kept this long. It struck him as extra funny when he pictured it through the eyes of a man like Réjean, and he began to chuckle himself. They stood laughing together at the roadside. He could still feel the impression of Réjean's hand on his arm as Réjean, still chuckling, stepped back from the muddy roadside just as a transport truck flew by, taking him along, pasted to the front grille.

Martin stood in the rain staring down the highway, paralyzed, the gun still cradled in his outstretched hand. He didn't know if other vehicles passed by during that time, whether it was still raining, what had just happened. But he knew that Réjean was no longer there. Most of Martin's body twisted west, searching down the road, as though he could see through time and space and the transport truck was still receding into the distance. He pictured Réjean's face and heard his laugh, the way he had said Martin's name. Not only had Réjean not made a big deal out of the Ford, he thought it was funny. Martin felt empty, like the transport truck had snatched away all his insides along with Réjean.

Although he could barely feel his legs, he shuffled up the shoulder and stood in the exact spot where Réjean had been struck, placing his considerably smaller feet in the impressions of Réjean's boots. He turned in a circle, taking it in: la route, les arbres, le ciel et la pluie. No Réjean. Anywhere. It seemed as though if he stayed there and kept looking, Réjean should materialize. But the thing he felt with absolute crystal certainty, in his marrow, was that Réjean was no more. He foggily recognized that he should call the police, but he lacked the capacity to put actions and ideas together. The world around him had grown white and empty, and as the rain spat loudly on his hat, he felt as though he were standing inside a yellow house, looking out a window at a world he was no longer a part of. He looked down at the gun in his palm. After some aimless fumbling, he managed to slide the gun under the flap of his pocket.

Martin glanced up and saw the Silverado sitting opposite him, but couldn't look directly back at it, as it implored him for answers he couldn't provide. Despite his stupor, he felt it was wrong to just climb into another man's truck, but convention was meaningless now. Martin shuffled toward the Silverado until his fingertip just touched the door handle, then tapped it, surprised to be making contact with something solid. He closed his eyes and hoisted himself into the other world of the Silverado.

Among the many traits Martin admired about Réjean, one of the greatest was his tidiness. Réjean's trade-ins were reliably returned in almost exactly the same condition he had bought them. Immaculate. They shared a love of order, but Martin felt Réjean wore it better. He stretched out his arms, laid both palms flat on the seats and caressed the upholstery. He was giving it a tender downward stroke when he noticed the brown paper bag. He reached down, then stopped. The truck was watching his every move, like a horse awaiting its fallen rider. His hand was hovering over the edge of the seat, halfway to the bag, when the reality of Réjean's non-existence hit him again, reminding him of the world where he now lived, alone. He lunged for the bag and pulled apart the folded flap. It was a full-size brown grocery bag containing a lunch that could have fed a few men. The void inside Martin cried out. He thrust in his hand and pulled out a big waxed-paper package. Sandwiches. Four of them. Four! He took out one and examined it. The bread was soft and visibly homemade, the slices incongruous, with a crust that was darker and coarser than you saw in the store, but the bread itself...He had never seen bread so fluffy or white. Two thick slices of baloney poked out from its edges. He caressed the sandwich thoughtfully, sniffed it, closed his eyes, and replayed over and over Réjean's big hand smacking his arm until he noticed he was squeezing the sandwich. Butter and plain yellow mustard oozed out around the slabs of baloney. Martin pictured the hand holding the knife that spread the butter and mustard, and panic began to simmer up from the chasm inside him. Without thinking, he stuffed half the sandwich into his mouth, breathing heavily as he chewed. He threw his head back against the seat and began to cry with his mouth closed, then stuffed the other half of the sandwich in his mouth and used his hand to hold the whole thing in. He dove for the Thermos on the passenger seat and tore the lid off, spilling coffee on himself. As it cascaded down his front, he snuffled in the wonderful dark smell. The aroma was rich, free of the industrial tang of the coffee at work. Jack Bureau had been a coffee drinker and Martin regretted never having been able to appreciate a beverage that smelled so good and for which his father had had such affection. He tilted his head back and opened his esophagus. He drank the wonderful smell, the smell of a house, the smell of a home. It wasn't scalding, but was hot enough to be *too* hot. Martin glugged some back up, the back of his throat burning, swished it around his palate, and let it wash back down. He wiped his mouth with his wet sleeve, smearing sandwich and coffee across his face, and dug his hand back in the bag. He pulled out another waxed-paper package, wider than it was tall, ripping apart one layer of paper and then the next to reveal the brown-sugar-sprinkled expanse of a dozen date squares. Martin pried one out, dropping the rest in his lap, and held it up to his face, smelling it and smelling it again. He squooshed the middle so that some of the dates squeezed out, then daintily bit around the edges to even the dates up with the crust and took one giant bite. Then two. He couldn't remember ever feeling so hungry.

The loss of Réjean made him feel that things were breaking up and drifting away outside of his control. Not just Réjean, but himself. He felt unwhole, unsolid, like his head and hands might float away like balloons. He stuffed another date square down his gullet, poured some more coffee into his mouth and down his chin, mingling with his tears, and forced down yet another date square. Then, breathing and gulping, he bunched up the lunch bag and dropped it on the floor, patted Colonel Weed's gun in his pocket, and slid numbly from the driver seat, not even thinking to close the door.

On a tattered gold sofa, Réjean awoke in tremendous pain, with most of his legs dangling over the sofa's arm. Through half-closed eyes, he first made out a purple wall, then a bearded man sitting in front of it in an armchair, smoking, reading a book with a sailboat on the cover. The gentle creak of the sofa springs snapped the man's attention from his page. He sucked in the remainder of his cigarette, crushed it out in a teeming ashtray, and, with a grunt of inconvenience, disappeared behind a velvet curtain.

Réjean felt the clutch of a bandage around his ribs. When he went to touch it, he discovered his hands enveloped in a pair of gauze mittens. He held them up in front of his face, unable to remember having gotten hurt. Surely, with enough inspection, they would reveal the source of the injury. He was swaddled in several layers of blankets and topped with a goose-down duvet.

The bearded man returned with a cup of tea on a saucer. Réjean turned over gingerly on his side and cringed from the strain. The man pulled a coffee table up next to the sofa and set down the tea. Réjean reached absurdly for the cup with his bandaged hands, but couldn't grasp it. The bearded man sat on the edge of the coffee table, lifted the cup to Réjean's lips, and tilted it just enough so that Réjean could slurp some off the top.

"Merci," said Réjean, sinking painfully back down to the divot created by his body.

The man rolled his eyes. "French..." he muttered, then glancing at Réjean's bandaged hands, slightly softened his tone. "You feel okay?"

Réjean shrugged and grimaced. "Qu'est ce qui m'est arrivé?" he asked, holding up his hands.

"Ah, you don't know," said the man.

Réjean shook his head.

"Well, I can't help you there. We found you, side of the road. You were lying in a ditch for a while. Maybe a few days. Smaller guy wouldn't have made it. You got roughed up bad though, tell you that."

Réjean thought hard, but came up with nothing like getting roughed up or lying in a ditch. He took his eyes on a trip around the room: the chipboard, the aimlessly suspended fabric, the Naugahyde bar, the nautical upright lamp behind the armchair where the bearded man had been reading. Réjean searched, but nothing had any meaning.

The man lit another cigarette and blew out the match. The smell of smoke provoked a warm familiarity in Réjean, and he watched as the plume dissipated in mid-air.

"Smoke?" said the man, and held out the white-and-gold pack, then looked at Réjean's bandaged hands and mumbled, "Oh." He took one out, lit it, and held it to Réjean's lips. Réjean sucked in the smoke as he had seen the man do and coughed it out violently, lifting a padded hand to his side to keep his ribcage from bursting open.

"Kay," said the man, placing the cigarette in the ashtray next to his own. He fed Réjean some more tea and alternately smoked both cigarettes himself. "The Colonel's out just now," he said, lifting the cup to Réjean's lips. Then, remembering it was the thing to do, he said, "I'm JC."

Réjean went to respond and couldn't. He came up empty. "Je m'appelle...Je m'appelle..." Nothing. He didn't know. He didn't know who he was. He didn't recognize his own body. He had been found at the side of the road like an old muffler.

Réjean recovered quickly at Colonel Weed's on a diet of organ meat, cheese, and wine, and soon began doing odd jobs around the compound. He was sterilizing a cheese vat when JC pulled up next to him in the Colonel's Dodge Dakota and said, "Hey, Serge, wanna go for a drive?"

Serge was the name the Colonel had given him, after a French singer he adored. The Colonel had always said that if he had had a son, that's what he would have named him. This was the role Réjean was gradually taking on. He and the Colonel would have long, laughing discussions that JC could only imagine must be about French itself; the new guy didn't know much else. But surely he must have been curious about his old life, whatever it was. Someone must have been looking for him. The Colonel had even offered to help, with the understanding that the police would not be notified. But as the weeks stretched on, and Réjean and the Colonel grew closer, Réjean's curiosity dwindled. He didn't have the feeling of there being something he needed to get back to. The Colonel encouraged the other men to include Serge in their regular activities and tried to impress upon them how much easier their jobs would be with him around. The men didn't care for new things, though, and had never had much luck making friends—they barely tolerated each other—but they were happy to unload the heavy lifting. When the Colonel suggested to JC that he take Réjean along on a payment run, he grudgingly agreed.

Réjean climbed into the Dakota and his eyes grew wide.

"You never been in a truck, Serge?" JC asked.

Réjean shook his head. "Ch'pense pas."

The shocks on the Dakota were bad. The Colonel swore that after this one, he would never buy another Dodge. From now on he would only buy Renaults.

JC decided to take the back road.

As they green-laned along at top speed, tumbling into potholes and careening over exposed tree roots, Réjean's head banged regularly against the roof as he grabbed for the handle over the window. JC smoked, grinning to himself. But Réjean soon got the hang of the bumps and stopped fighting the momentum that bounced him out of his seat. He watched the trees as they zipped out of sight, turning to catch them in the rear window as they passed, receding into the distance.

JC took an exit off the main road into a lot where a butter-coloured mobile home sat behind a lit-up sign that spelled *WORLD OF CHEESE*.

"This guy moves a lot of our stuff," said JC. "But he's an idiot and he never shuts up. He'll do anything he can not to pay, but he's got the busiest cheese shop in three townships.

I always try and make these quick. See if you can look like you mean business. He's gonna want to talk."

As they approached the store, the man could be seen through the window gesticulating at a female customer with a wrapped wedge of cheese. JC rolled his eyes.

"*Look* at him," he said, stopping and lighting another cigarette. "He stands there all day long, talking. I've never seen him *not* talking." JC glowered through the window a moment longer and let out a huff. "Idiot," he muttered.

When they walked in the door, the man fluttered to attention and handed the wedge of cheese to the woman, who grabbed it and fled.

"Mr. JC! What a wonderful surprise! What can I get you? I just baked biscuits this morning with some of your paysan, though I had to bake them at home because I'm still fighting to get a food-prep permit and I can't even tell you the trouble they're giving me. I had to cart three dozen biscuits and muffins across town in the Corolla and, well, I don't know if you've seen the trunks in those things. You can see it out there right now. Just right out there. It's the gold one. Look at that, it's just a tiny hatchback thing and I have to pile pans of biscuits on top of each other and they get all mashed up, which is not good for presentation. You know, if I could bake on-site, I could use more of your cheese. I mean, if you knew anyone you could talk to on council, anyone at all, I'll bet they'd listen. With me they're just like, well, I scare them or something. That's their problem, you know. They're afraid of new ideas."

JC lit a cigarette and threw his match on the floor. The man went on.

"I'm thinking of opening up a patio out front. Have I told you about this? I'm going to hire local jazz musicians and have, like, soirées. Have I mentioned this? So obviously, I'm going to be moving a lot of cheese, but I'm also looking at having the patio licensed, so I could be moving a lot of wine, too, if you know what I mean?" He gave JC a theatrical look. "Only thing is, you know how the town council is with liquor licences. I don't know if you've ever tried getting a licence in this town, but..."

Réjean, initially dumbfounded by the onslaught of chatter, remembered he was supposed to look like he meant business, and took a step forward. The cheese idiot fell silent, moved straight to the till, and started stuffing cash into a yellow envelope.

JC took the paved roads home.

Sitting at his kitchen table, Martin patted his coat pocket. Gun, he thought, and a warm surge of affection swept through him. He was also comforted by the smattering of crumbs stuck to the front of his coat. Certainly, he had eaten a date square before, but these ones were different. They were not only unusually delicious, but had an intangible familiarity to them, and a hint of lemon peel. They felt almost alive in his guts.

Carrés de dattes, he thought. Carrés de dattes.

With his hand on his belly, he repeated the words to himself until a pan of date squares materialized in the air before him. *Carrés de dattes.* A pair of red oven mitts appeared beneath the pan, carrying it toward him. Slowly and fuzzily at first, then more clearly, two arms appeared from the ends of the oven mitts, leading to a pair of shoulders and a sleeveless pantsuit. Atop the pantsuit was the warm face of a woman with golden hair, tied up in a big braided bun, like a brioche. A woman who loved Réjean Lapointe. A woman who shared his truck and his home and his bed. Though he hadn't been denying her existence entirely, Martin had been pushing her from his mind more than he was willing to admit. Something itched at him that he couldn't place. There was plenty itching at him, in fact, but he had lost the presence of mind to sift through it, and sat at the table until dawn, studying the linoleum, hoping for clarity.

When the morning sun shone through the gauzy curtains left by the previous tenant, Martin got an impulse. He stood up from the table and waited for the next one. This was good. This was easy. Impulses would tell him what came next. Impulse moved him to the door and into the Ranger.

His appearance at the dealership cast a confused hush over the sales guys, who watched him from the main building as he parked what was unmistakably a Ford Ranger and emerged from it wearing what was definitely a set of yellow foul-weather gear. It wasn't raining. They watched in disconcerted silence as he walked straight past the building to his portable, disappeared through the plywood door, and reappeared with his name-tag pinned to his raincoat. His journey to the middle of the car lot looked exploratory.

A woman with three straggling kids approached him and, without seeming to notice his attire, began to tell him what she was looking for. She had just received a big divorce settlement and custody of the kids. She was determined to buy a family sport utility vehicle that day, take the kids up to stay with her parents, and go on a trip by herself. She needed to get away. Martin had these ones down cold. Normally, he started by demonstrating his solemn approval of her situation by showing, with a softening of his face, his appreciation of the weight of her decision. Then he would veer gently away from her anger, without dismissing it, by moving on to the lighter topic of the kids themselves and how much work they must be; he would include an observation along the lines of "Bet they keep you on your toes" or "They sure look like a handful." It was important to let moms know he understood what a difficult job they had. But today Martin came up with nothing. He couldn't imagine anything more unnatural than talking to a stranger.

As he waited for his next impulse, he looked down at the older of her boys, who was playing with two toy soldiers, making *pheeoo* sounds with his lips. Martin turned all his attention to the child and his soldiers.

"I'm thinking red. What do you have that's red?" asked the woman.

Martin looked up from the child and said, "I gotta go," turned sharply, and headed for the Ranger with a quick, rigid gait. He knew he needed to be near Réjean's wife, but he hadn't yet retrieved the reason why from the mess inside him. He climbed in and gunned the engine, peeling across the lot as his co-workers at the window gaped. Ferris ran out the door to grab the sale.

He knew where the Lapointe house was from Réjean's documentation, and had on many occasions driven past the end of the long, wooded driveway, where the number 1739 was burned into a varnished wooden plaque hanging from a post. He parked the Ranger a safe distance away from the foot of the drive, which went up a steep, winding incline, receding into the trees. You couldn't see the house at all from the road. He raised his elbows as he tiptoed through the leaves, believing it made him lighter. When he reached the bend in the drive and saw the house, he stopped again. She would be inside, in her red oven mitts. The idea of being close to her filled him with a sparkly excitement.

Martin crept along the side of the house until he saw the front door. The lights were on in the kitchen and a round little woman sat at the table in a track suit, smoking. She wore no brioche bun or oven mitts. His eyes locked on her and he could not tear them away. With tiny, invisible steps, he edged toward the wooded back area under the black canopy of pine. From this vantage point through the kitchen window, he could watch her clearly.

"Agathe," he said. He'd never spoken her name out loud, and realized that all this time he'd only referred to her with Réjean as "your wife."

Every so often her shoulders would lift and her head and neck would wrench forward in a froggy sort of way, like she was forcing her eyes open. She put out her cigarette, downed whatever was in her cup, and put on her coat. Martin held his breath as she opened the door and passed him in the trees, heading for the road.

Martin slunk down the drive and saw her stand at the bus stop. He followed her all day as she put up posters of Réjean, and showed their wedding photo to strangers, asking if they'd seen him. At night, once Martin saw her safely in the house, he crept back down to the road and slept in his truck. He could think of no other place he wanted to be.

When his eyes flicked open, Martin oriented himself immediately and remembered why he was sleeping in the truck. He crept back up to the window of the kitchen where Agathe was again at the table, smoking and drinking tea, about to make her way down to the bus stop.

Martin never returned to work. Not only did he feel tethered to Agathe for reasons he couldn't explain, but the idea of spending a day selling cars to strangers now seemed absurd. He couldn't believe he had been doing it all this time. After three months, bills would pile up on his untended doorstep and his landlady would call again and again, hoping he was okay. She would hold his apartment for those three months out of gratitude for his expert recommendation of her Chevy Cavalier, until she was forced to rent the apartment to a new tenant and put his belongings out on the street.

One day, Martin followed Agathe to Convenience Place Mall, where she often put up posters and asked people about having seen Réjean. But on this day, she walked in to Stereoblast and stayed there for over an hour. When she didn't come out, Martin wondered if she had left without his noticing. He hadn't seen anyone come or go, and despite his discomfort, he decided to go in and check.

The song of the door sensor and the sight of her in a real-life tableau with other humans stopped Martin in his tracks. She was holding a bucket full of brightly coloured rags in one hand and a yellow feather duster in the other. Two men stood with her, an older one in a shirt and tie and a younger one with a round, curly helmet of hair. They all looked up when he walked in, leaving him frozen at the door. He lowered the brim of his hat and moved to the nearest rack, displaying hot curler sets and other hair-styling appliances.

The older man continued to Agathe, "We figure, people come in, they see you cleaning, they know we really care about quality. You seem pretty serious, and that's good. 'Stereoblast: we're serious about quality.'"

The curly-haired man laughed and twirled a lock of his hair on his finger. "Good one," he said, nodding.

Agathe smiled stiffly.

"Serious about quality," said Wood.

"Yeah," said Tony.

"When we opened up in '83, you should have seen the place. Just a few display cases and some modular shelving. Now, look at these walls. What do you see?"

When no one answered, the curly-haired guy said, "Gently used appliances and electronics?"

"Yeah, but what do they hang on?"

"Hooks!"

"Okay, but where do you hang the hooks?"

"The walls?"

"Right, but what's covering the walls?"

"Gently used…"

"Pegboard, Tony. It takes a managerial eye to see that. The walls are covered in holes, every hole can support a hook, every hook can hang a piece of merchandise. Know why? Coz Carl Turcott, Mr. Stereoblast himself, calls me up one day and says, 'Debow, I've seen your numbers. I've seen how that store is going and I like it. Tell you what, I'm thinking we double the volume of that place.' You know why he said that?"

"Why," asked Tony.

"Coz he knew I could handle it. You don't give a man perforated pegboard walls, you don't think he can sell what's hanging on 'em. And I can sell what's hanging on 'em. Which is why he called."

Agathe was deeply lost in thought, fluffing gently at the air with her yellow duster.

She emerged at the end of the day, and Martin followed her bus home. He repeated the trip, tailing her to her job the next day and every day thereafter without question. For reasons he still didn't understand, he could not leave her alone.

What he had gained by ducking out of the world was a

newfound dryness. Sitting inside his home of foul-weather gear, he would lightly flutter his arms to feel the way the air passing through no longer chilled the wet parts of him, but simply breezed along his sides as though rustling through dead grass.

He was becoming increasingly resourceful with respect to his own survival, learning how to use newspaper to cushion and cover his sleep. Mealtimes, or the times when his emptiness was too painful to ignore, he would go through the Dumpsters at Convenience Place, find the thing that smelled least awful, and stuff down enough of it to satisfy the shrinking space in his abdomen.

At four in the afternoon, Colpitt's Grocery dumped the day's unsellable produce, and Dingwall's Donuts put out the stale pastries just after nine, when they closed. Even though it was during his evening watch, Martin would race back to the mall for the Dingwall's deposit. The value of the soft, pastry-filled garbage bag was worth the risk; it not only smelled good and served Martin for several meals, but was also good to sleep on. He dreamed of eclairs.

While he was able to handle food and shelter on his own, he still needed money for gas to follow Agathe to and from work. The day Martin spent his last cent on gas, he parked the Ranger at Convenience Place, stepped down, and crossed the parking lot to the front doors, where he stood until a man approached. When the man got near enough, Martin opened the door and held out his hand. The man looked surprised, but rummaged in his pocket, came up with some loose change, and dropped it into Martin's palm. Martin nodded and pocketed the change. Effortless.

The mall had no other panhandlers, so Martin had the market cornered, although he was making more money than he intended. He would stretch out to sleep on the front seat of the Ranger and coins poured out of his pockets.

Inevitably, he one day found himself holding the door for Agathe. He had been watching her approach from under the brim of his hat, not sure what to do when she reached him. He didn't want her money. He opened the door without putting out his hand, hoping she would walk on, but she stopped and dug in her purse, pulled out a loonie and handed it to him. Still concealed by his hat, he shook his head. She stood solid, loonie extended. Martin took a step back.

"Décide-toi, là," she said, pocketing the coin and walking on. Now every time she passed through the door, she ignored him and he nodded, glad she didn't insist.

They continued this manoeuvre as though they had decided on it together, until the blond woman with the big blue parka got hired at Stereoblast, and things changed. She and Agathe were driving to work together—Agathe was driving them to work in the Honda Civic. She no longer took her breaks at Hickey's. She spent a lot of time with the blond woman now, smoking on the loading dock, talking, and laughing. Raucously. Agathe laughed a lot.

Friday night, as Martin was waiting for Agathe to finish the vacuuming, she and the blond woman suddenly ran out the door and jumped into the Civic, as though escaping from captivity. Martin threw the Ranger into gear and pulled out behind them, trying to keep a suitable distance between the two vehicles. The Civic pulled into the parking lot of a roadhouse, and Martin followed them through the door into the pulsing room. Locked in the crowd, he couldn't move of his own free will in any direction, only where the crowd took him. He abandoned himself to the tide, but kept the halo of the blond woman's hair in sight as a beacon.

A man nudged him against the current of bodies, and with friendly recognition, said, "Hey." Martin tried to place him as the man was reabsorbed by the wall of people. He didn't know him. Other people occasionally showed signs of recognition as well. It took him some time to understand that he had opened the door for them. He lowered his hat, believing it made him less conspicuous.

He watched as the blond woman finagled seats at the bar from two young men and struck up a conversation with them while Agathe let her eyes linger where they landed. She seemed to be sitting up straighter.

As the loud song playing died down, there was a change in the air. The banging and shouting was taken over by a tinkling electronic piano, and couples started filtering off toward the dance floor. As the flow propelled him toward the back of the room, he spotted a man sitting all by himself at a table in an alcove. Though it was dark, he could make out the outline of the man's square-brimmed military cap and a long, aquiline nose. He wouldn't have looked twice had the man not begun shouting to an imaginary foe. Martin looked harder now. The man was wearing a set of military fatigues, and seemed to be watching Agathe.

Agathe took a sip of beer and closed her eyes with what looked like relief. She appeared uncharacteristically at home.

When Martin checked back to where the man sat, he found him turned so he was facing Agathe, shouting at her. When the music got a little louder, the man pointed at her and shouted even louder, using the muscles in his face. Fear flooded Martin's whole body as the pieces dropped into place. This was the man from the Lobster Shack Réjean had told him about. This man wanted to hurt Agathe. He was threatening her right now, and was so close he could walk right across the bar and touch her. Martin patted his pocket for the Colonel's gun. Agathe couldn't know the danger sitting so close by, but she seemed to be watching him from behind the blond woman's hair. Martin readied himself by clenching and unclenching his fists. She was definitely looking; in fact, she was *sneaking* looks.

The man was getting agitated and shaking his fist. Who knew how crazy he might get? Why were people not fleeing? Martin reached his hand slowly inside his pocket flap, his eyes never leaving the man's face, and he began to notice symmetry between the man's babbling and the music playing. Agathe was equally rapt. No. She was more than that. It was like they were aware of each other. It was when he pointed again at Agathe that Martin's mind emptied like an hourglass and he watched, slack-mouthed.

Baybay-eeyay-eeyayay, oo I get chills when I'm with you, ohwhoawhoa ohwhoawhoa.

They *were* aware of each other. The man was. Singing. To her.

The wind drained from Martin's lungs as he gathered the information. Of course. Looking on now that he knew the man wasn't crazy, what struck Martin most of all, aside from his emotional commitment to his performance, was that he clearly didn't give a single thought to what other people thought of him. The man had probably never broken a sweat.

"Hey, Crazy Yellow Guy! No way!" said the blond woman, craning her neck just past Agathe.

Martin suddenly felt painfully embarrassed. He was not only unneeded, he was also unwanted, or he would be if either Agathe or the army man knew he was there. Which they didn't. Because no one cared whether he was there or not. His face burned.

Martin looked at the man one last time as the couples returned to their tables. Just before they obscured him like a curtain, the man gulped down the rest of his beer and slipped through the crowd to the door.

Martin couldn't help himself now. Knowing that Agathe was in no danger, he followed the man out to the parking lot, holding back to let him cover some distance before following. The army man buttoned his coat and rifled in his pocket for his keys, climbing into a Ford F-100. When Martin got close enough to the truck to see through the half-open window, he stopped. The man was putting the key in the ignition, laughing to himself. Spotting Martin so close, so clearly looking, he stuck his head out the window and said, "Crazy Yellow Guy! Can I help you, brother?"

Martin said, "You were...singing to a woman in there."

The man laughed. "Yeah," he said.

Helplessly awed, Martin said, "Do you...Do you know her?"

"Naw," he said. "Naw, not really. But, I don't know. She's the only one who noticed me in there, and it's fun to have somebody to sing to." He looked seriously at Martin. "I love to sing, man."

Martin nodded, dumbfounded.

"I'll tell you, though, it was a stupid thing to do. Her boy-friend is huge. I'm lucky he wasn't there, or I'd be dead." He laughed again. "That guy wants to kill me."

As he watched the man drive away, Martin acknowledged that somewhere in his heart, through the loss and obscurity, he knew Agathe didn't need him. And somewhere in there, he didn't care. But when he got the full impact of his irrelevance, it became all-consuming. He felt ill-formed. Amorphous. He was a ghost, a coward, and a rotten friend—the only area in which he had ever really wanted to excel. It was too much to think about.

He drove back to the mall and parked out by the Dumpsters. Right on time, the Dingwall's manager brought out the stale-pastry bag. Martin hefted it from the bin to the Ranger and placed it on the passenger seat. He untied the top and pulled out an apple fritter, then dropped it back in the bag. The emptiness inside him no longer felt like a space that needed filling, but like a depleted granary with only the remaining chaff waiting to be swept out. He tied the bag and pushed the top down with his hand. The air whistled out like a slow, sad song.

Agathe waved the bus on as it passed her at the stop. As she watched for Debbie, she squinted, waiting for the gleaming white Civic to burst through the grey around it. Debbie was late. Normally, Agathe could hear the Civic coming, and now listened carefully. When the Civic finally did appear, it didn't announce itself at all. Debbie was also unusually quiet when she slid out of the driver side to let Agathe in. Agathe noticed that T-Rex was playing, and she turned it up. But Debbie only half-smiled, which seemed to be for Agathe's benefit.

"C'est le petit," said Agathe.

Debbie didn't respond.

"Y'a-t-il quelque chose?" Agathe asked, her hand anticipatorily poised on the gearshift.

Debbie clicked her tongue. "Aw, hon," she said. "I applied for a job with the company Blaine and Sebastian work for, and just found out last night that I got it."

"Ah!" said Agathe.

"It's in the city," said Debbie.

"Ah," said Agathe.

Blaine and Sebastian from the Whisky Mak hadn't realized they were teaching Debbie Visual Basic until she was sitting on a kitchen chair drinking Baileys in Sebastian's bedroom, and taking notes. Every night she would show up unannounced, but overwhelmingly welcome. She got herself certified, and when an entry-level position opened up at the software company where Blaine and Sebastian worked, Debbie marched in for the interview and marched out their first-ever female computer programmer.

"I start in a couple of weeks," said Debbie, "but I have to move. I'm going to tell Wood this morning." She paused. "I have to start packing and looking for a place, so this'll probably be my last day."

Agathe knew that Debbie had been learning about computer programming for the past few months, but she hadn't stopped to wonder why anyone would learn a skill in order to keep working at Stereoblast.

"Dans la ville," said Agathe.

"Yeah," said Debbie.

Agathe concertedly shifted the car into gear and pulled onto the road, waiting for the acceleration to lift her spirits. When it didn't, she went faster.

"On va au drive-thru?" she asked, pulling into the passing lane.

"Hell, yeah," said Debbie.

Agathe passed every car on the way to Dingwall's, carrying on a battle inside her head. She didn't want to want Debbie to stay, and if there was one thing she was learning, it was that sometimes people went away, and that being sad about it made no difference. Pushing forward was the only option. It wasn't as though she wanted Debbie to keep working at Stereoblast; she wouldn't wish that on anyone.

"Deux gros thé avec crème," said Agathe into the drive-thru speaker.

"Bag in!" shouted Debbie from the passenger seat, stuffing a bill into Agathe's hand. Agathe was too sad to fight.

Back on the road, Debbie said, "I don't know, Agathe, this town..."

"C'est un town full of losers."

"That's right," Debbie laughed. "I'm pullin' outta here to win."

"Pullin' outta here to win..." said Agathe to the dashboard.

"You know," said Debbie. "Bruce is just saying what he knows we all feel. About needing something new. There's so much stuff out there, and we only get to see the tiniest bit of it. It's right to want more." She paused. "Coz maybe tomorrow the good lord'll take you away." She sipped her tea and lit a cigarette. "You know, you might like the city. Have you ever even been there? There's rock-and-roll shows all the time. I can get you a job. We can go see the Pretenders."

Agathe nodded, knowing she was staying right here.

"You know it's never too late. It's never too late for anything. I mean, how much longer can you really wait for him to come back?"

"Ché pas..." Agathe said, knowing that she did. "Ché pas...E could come home asoir." She turned to see if she had convinced Debbie.

She knew could just go. She and Debbie could go see the Pretenders. But she also knew in her fort intérieur she wasn't finished here, and that only she would know when it was time. Point final.

"Ben, félicitations, ton job," said Agathe. "C'est excitant."

"I'm gonna miss you," said Debbie.

"Oui," said Agathe. "I'm gonna miss you, too."

Without meaning to, Réjean had started growing a long, blunt beard. No one said anything about it, it just happened. As he eased into a life working for the Colonel, Réjean gradually stopped wondering what he was missing in the life he'd left. He was learning the intricacies of cheese and wine, and spending large parts of his day intimidating people. Not only did he enjoy the work, but he was really improving productivity. He had streamlined the pickup process, earning the respect of JC, who would laugh the whole way back to the truck every time they left a client's shop.

He was learning that it was common for their dealers to try and avoid paying what they owed, and it baffled him. The shopkeepers had received the product and sold it for a profit, yet still looked for ways around paying the Colonel his cut. The Colonel was a fair man and produced magnificent cheese. It made no sense that people would want to steal from him. After all the Colonel had done for Réjean, he felt a particular contempt for people trying to cheat him. Réjean had no patience for excuses, and no one made excuses like the cheese idiot. Since their first meeting and his well-placed fear of Réjean, his belief in his own charm was making him feel comfortable again, and he had reverted to his old ways of delaying payment with chatter. Réjean felt more and more agitated every time they went to see him.

The idiot's envelopes had been light for the past few pickups, just a little each time, until the Colonel was officially unhappy and sent Réjean and JC to make it right. The Colonel kept himself away from the dealers, restricting his time to things he enjoyed. He had never met the cheese idiot, but when JC tried to describe his infuriating manner, the Colonel only looked at him with calm, expectant eyes. He didn't like excuses either. If the idiot didn't want to pay, his men would have to find a way to make him—with minimal violence. Although the Colonel sold guns as a side business to supplement the cheese and wine, he thought it gauche to use them on the job.

When they pulled up to the front door, the idiot was again talking with a customer. Réjean got a good look at him through the window and felt a new irritation bubbling up in his chest.

JC had scheduled this trip just before closing time so that there would be no customers around, in case things got serious. But the idiot was blithely detaining the customer and seemed to have no interest in closing.

When JC and Réjean walked through the door, he flew into gear.

"Heyyyyyyyyyyy! These are some of the guys who make my fabulous cheeses! This must be so exciting for you," he said to the customer, who had already slipped out the door. Réjean turned the lock, and the idiot fell mute. The silence permeated Réjean's nerves, but he waited for a cue from JC, who lit a cigarette off his last one, crushed out the butt on the floor, and said, "I don't need to tell you. And I'm not gonna."

The idiot dove under the counter and emerged brandishing a cheese knife. "Don't come near me," he screeched, stabbing at the air with the knife.

He held the knife aloft for a moment from behind the

counter, then made a break for the door. Réjean felt a sharp pain in his shoulder and looked into the terrified eyes of the idiot, who was struggling to pull the knife free.

Reflexively, Réjean picked him up by the throat and held him in mid-air, his legs scrambling. With one big hand around his neck, Réjean gave him a shake. Just one. The sound was like a hollow knock.

Réjean released the idiot, quickly reaching out to catch the body and support the head as it lolled gently back and to the right. He felt for a pulse and put his ear to the idiot's mouth to check for air. Nothing. Réjean looked to JC, whose cigarette dangled from his motionless fingers.

Still capable of practicality, JC went first to the cash register and pounded buttons until the drawer opened up, then emptied it out and headed into the back office.

Réjean gathered up the body and held it close, still waiting for guidance from JC, who was rustling in the back room as the idiot cooled in Réjean's arms.

JC came out stuffing handfuls of cash into World of Cheese bags and said, "Okay," trying not to let on that this was the first dead person he had ever seen. "Okay, Serge. I'm...I know. That...wasn't supposed to..."

Réjean looked around for somewhere to set down the body.

"Serge," said JC.

Réjean knelt down, lay the body across his lap, and gazed into the dull eyes.

"Serge. Serge buddy, we gotta go."

Réjean slid the body from his arms and crouched unsteadily beside it. "Chus tellement sorry," Réjean said, partially hoping for a response as he straightened out the legs and crossed the hands on the idiot's chest. He tried to straighten the head, too, but it lay impossibly tilted.

Agathe stood smoking, her eyes roaming the curves of the Silverado. It was her first day without Debbie, and she had no intention of taking the bus. Ever again. She stubbed out her cigarette in the can by the door, slipped her finger through the loop of the key chain, and swung the keys around into her palm. She remembered how Réjean used to constantly play with these keys, absently tossing them in the air or shaking them like dice. It used to drive her crazy, but she was beginning to appreciate the connection you could have with a set of car keys.

She climbed into the driver seat and snuggled her back into the soft velour of the upholstery, enforcing her own presence.

There was close to a metre between her feet and the pedals. She scrabbled underneath the seat until she found the handle and moved herself smoothly forward and back, adjusting to suit her body. She slid the big Chevrolet key into the ignition and gently brought her foot down on the pedal.

The Silverado wasn't so different from Debbie's Civic. She concentrated on the steps: clutch, neutral, key, release, clutch, first. The engine coughed once before kicking in, and the sound of it made the hairs on her arms stand up. It felt like she was bringing a dead thing back to life, which made her shudder. She remembered the heater and reached for the knob, savouring the familiar click. There was a strange smell to the air, like dusty fatigue, but it burned off after a minute and she relaxed completely into the truck's warm cocoon.

She reached her hands out to the steering wheel and rested her head against the back of the seat.

Just underneath the heater was the radio, once a source of such irritation. She clicked it on and jerked back her hand at the sound of "Viens voir l'Acadie." It was like the voice of a ghost. As she touched the dial to change it, she felt just a hint of sympathy for the song; it had no rhythm or build, no smashing crescendo, no torment, no sonofabitch, but it was pretty in an innocent way. She turned the dial.

There was buzzing, then talking, then static, buzzing, a classical orchestra, buzzing, talking, then a big, loud guitar. Like a machine gun. It was the Guess Who, singing about the American woman they wished would leave them alone. This one came after you just like the barracuda. She turned it up, filling the truck with noise.

Once on the road, the Silverado sped smoothly through the blowing snow, lifting her miles off the ground so that she was looking down at the other cars. When she swished by them in the passing lane, she imagined they were the little fish and she was the barracuda, devouring them one by one.

Agathe cut the engine outside of Stereoblast and again relaxed into the upholstery, leaving the key in the ignition for the radio. The wind whipped around the Silverado, blowing in swirls around the parking lot.

She lit a cigarette and reached for her tea, which was wedged between the seats in one of her own kitchen mugs; she made better tea than Dingwall's, and the drive-thru didn't feel right without Debbie. As she contemplated the storefront, she snuggled back deeper and rested her sneakered foot alongside the gearshift. The inside of the Silverado was warm as a bed. This was the kind of storm where people stayed home from work, and as much as she would have preferred that, one of the unexpected results of driving the Silverado to work was that it created a sort of bridge between the house and Stereoblast, making her feel almost like she hadn't left home. Not having to wait for Debbie at the bus stop had given her more time this morning, so that she could sit in the truck awhile longer before having to go into the store. She didn't feel like getting out right away.

The song on the radio faded out and an electronic keyboard piped in. Agathe laughed and turned it up as Sheriff told her they'd never needed love like they needed her.

As the song filled the cab, she closed her eyes and really listened. Even though it was a slow one, she was beginning to think this was a good song. And it really did pick up toward the end. She liked the athletic key change, and the way the drums announced the Baby. She listened to the whole thing as her cigarette extinguished from inattention. When she rolled down the window to pitch it, the wind raged in and she leaned out to feel the snow pelting her face. The walk from the truck to the store was fewer than thirty paces. One warm door to another. She hopped down and strode through the storm and through the front doors of Stereoblast.

Tony and Wood were standing in eerie silence near the cash, each listlessly propped on a Mandio. Neither looked up. A strand of Tony's hair fell forward from behind his ear and hung there, untucked.

Although she missed Debbie powerfully, a reserve of happiness cushioned Agathe from falling too low. What Debbie had given her fortified her like a new set of senses. Debbie had taught her how the sound of the E Street Band was the sound of Clarence Clemmons playing a little bit, all the time, even when you thought he wasn't. She'd taught her how Eric Clapton is called Slowhand because his fingers barely move even when he's playing something complicated. She had showed her how the verb tense of the choruses in "Had Me a Real Good Time" change throughout the song from when Rod Stewart shows up at the party to when he gets asked to leave, to show that time is passing. Debbie'd taught her how syncopation flips the song over and plays the opposite beat, and how a seventh sounds like the sun is bursting through the clouds. From the outside, Agathe couldn't have understood what those songs were made of; now that she was on the inside, she knew exactly what made the army man point and sing.

"We're closing today," said Tony. "It's the storm."

It was not the storm; it was Debbie. Wood's heartsick expression said as much.

What Agathe really wanted to do with a day like this was go for a drive, a good, long one, and shout along to the radio. But the storm was already bad and was expected to last for days. Un ice storm. She needed to stock up and get home— and when she pictured herself at home, warm, with tea, she remembered Sondage, sitting on the kitchen table. But an evening filling out a survey somehow didn't hold the same excitement anymore. Perhaps she would draw a picture. She also thought what she might do on a day like this was something she hadn't done since Réjean: she would cook. She would make a meal like the ones she used to make for him and fill the house with the smell of love. And she would eat it all. Herself. She would make a rappie pie, because it was fussy and would take hours, first cooking the chicken, then grating the potatoes and squeezing the liquid out of them in a cloth bag until they attained that glossy consistency. She might even get herself some beer.

She headed back toward the front doors of the mall, passing Crazy Yellow Guy. He was hard to miss even with the poor visibility. With the exception of seeing him at the Whisky Mak, he'd become a welcome omission from her day since she'd started taking her breaks with Debbie rather than at Hickey's. When she approached, he didn't even try to open the door. He just stood there. He looked different. Narrower. It was like he was fading away. He must have been a real person before he went crazy. He must have had a family. She reached past him for the door.

The stock at Colpitt's had been thoroughly picked over, but she still managed to get a chicken, dinner rolls, a bag of potatoes, and onions.

She swooshed back out the front door and was struck by the gale. Crazy Yellow Guy was now curled up in a fetal position on the sidewalk, clutching his knees. Agathe looked around at the shoppers heading for shelter, then down at him, huddled on the ground, his back rounded like an armadillo. No. Not like an armadillo. No, what he unmistakably resembled, and what she hadn't devoted a guilty thought in some time to, was a brown bat curled up in the bottom of his cage. She set down her groceries, flipped up the collar of her coat, and turned him over. He opened his eyes just barely, then wider, before they rolled back in his head. Agathe hefted him over her shoulder and found him light, as though perforated. As she carried him to the truck, the Colonel's gun fell unseen from its home in his yellow pocket and into the slush.

Two weeks later, Tony would be murmuring to himself when he'd kick the gun out from a snowbank and across the icy lot. He would chase it under a Pontiac 6000. On his knees, the side of his face on the ground, he would lay his hand on the cold metal, pull it out, and say, "Wow."

The first thing Martin noticed when he woke up in the thick dark was the scent. It was like waking up inside another person, and the lingering musk of aftershave alerted him that that person was Réjean.

Martin was in a bed, covered by his own weight in quilts and scratchy blankets. The wind howled outside, whipping sheets of precipitation against the window. His muscles were rubbery, and lifting the bulky covers was a chore, but when he realized what he was wearing, he sank back on the pillows, dizzy. Even in his weakened state, he knew it was Réjean's shirt—although on Martin it was more like a nightgown. It wasn't just the smell, he knew the plaid and texture from memory. It *felt* like Réjean. As he drifted, in-haling deep lungfuls, Agathe appeared at the door in the halo of an emergency candle.

"Aie, you awake?" she said.

"Oui," he said.

She disappeared, reappearing a moment later with a but-tered white dinner roll. Martin watched her hazily as she nudged her hip in next to him on the bed. Dazzled by her closeness, he scuffled over as best he could to accommo-date her. The warmth of her flank radiated through him as she placed the roll in his hand and held up the candle to watch him.

"Mange donc, là. T'es starving," she said.

He couldn't remember the last thing that had passed through his lips. It could have been a month ago. He re-mained ambivalent to food, but would have eaten a boot if she had brought him one. He lifted the roll to his mouth and nibbled as she watched gravely. In the candle's glow, he was struck by the protuberance of her eyes. His stomach gripped with refusal as he forced down the last buttery bite

133

and chewed industriously, dipping his head to swallow.

She studied him with a scientific curiosity, as one might a bug or a rock. "As-tu un nom, toi?"

"Martin," he said. "Je m'appelle Martin."

"Martin," she said, pronouncing it the way Réjean did, with the emphasis on the last syllable. No one had spoken his name since he'd last seen Réjean, and he had to stop himself from asking her to say it again.

Satisfied, she left the room, the red smudge of the flame lingering in the blackness. He could hear her moving down the hall, the clatter of dishes. She returned a moment later with a giant plate of rappie pie, which she set down in his lap before reassuming the warmed spot next to him on the bed. Martin's esophagus ached. The roll alone had been more than he could handle, but he would not refuse her. She had brought him a spoon, perhaps unsure what he might do with a fork. He dug into the mountain of chicken and glistening potato and steadied himself with his other hand. He had to focus intently on chewing, sifting and settling the flavours on his tongue, gulping it down and, crucially, keeping it down, not distracting himself with stealing glances at her in the candlelight.

She watched him calmly as he stuffed down two heaping spoonfuls before his insides forced him to stop. He squeezed his eyes shut. He had been fading away bit by bit, week by week. The padding that protected his insides had melted away and he was nothing now but thin, empty skin. The introduction of food kicked into gear systems that had been closing down, and there was chaos in his innards.

With deep regret, he placed the spoon on the plate and handed it back to her, shaking his head. "Je m'excuse," he said.

"Ben, on fait ce qu'on peut," she said, not even treating him like an Anglophone. She firmly patted down the bedding around him, poking it under on all sides as he lay still, blissful and obedient. Once he was mummified, the covers up to his chin, she turned off the light and disappeared with the plate.

The room started to swirl as he gazed up at the ceiling. He pulled the covers over his head, hoping the darkness would stop the spinning, but it only made it worse. He was drunk with food. He took shallow, panting breaths and concentrated on not throwing up or passing out. But even as his insides sounded frenzied alarms, Martin at last felt fully, resoundingly solid.

Over the next six days, the town was besieged with rain, wind, and sub-zero temperatures that glazed every surface with a sheet of ice and made it nearly impossible to leave the house without a pair of skates. Power lines froze and the weight of the ice knocked them to the ground. Agathe was grateful for the gas stove that enabled her to continue cooking for Martin as he recovered. She slept next to the fireplace, waking up every few hours to pile on more wood, check on Martin, and tuck him in tighter. She sat with him as he slept and watched his face for fresh colour and the benefits of her care.

The first few days Martin slept straight through, waking only when Agathe would nudge him to eat. For someone who was crazy, he didn't act very crazy. In fact, he only behaved oddly one time, when he was finally well enough to sit up and she had arranged an area for him in the living room by the fireplace, tucked him in under three quilts, and brought him a cup of tea with cream and a date square.

He gave her his usual look of apologetic gratitude and was about to bite into the date square when he stopped it halfway to his mouth. His shoulders sank, and he looked tenderly at the square and squeezed it gently so a little of the filling crept out. Still holding it, his frame began to shake. He cried quietly while she sat by. He placed the date square back on its plate, sat straight up, looked her in the face, and took a breath to speak, then glanced back down at the plate, shook his head, and set the plate on the coffee table. Agathe went to the kitchen and returned with a pad of paper, a pencil, and a deck of cards.

"Voila, là," she said. "On joue le gin rummy."

Martin was quick to pick up gin rummy and they began playing endlessly. It provided some structure for their time together. Agathe played the battery-powered radio, and every time the room hummed with something unsaid, she would tell him what was on.

"Aerosmith, ça."

Within a few days, Martin was walking around and helping Agathe in the kitchen. He cleaned every dish she used, arranged the glassware according to height, and dusted the knick-knacks.

When the ice began to melt and the town emerged, hands on hips, many homes remained without power, but Stereoblast was back up and running right away. Agathe left Martin with a refrigerator full of leftovers and went reluctantly back to work.

There was no denying that things just weren't the same without Debbie. The coffee tasted thin and bitter, and Tony couldn't remember if he had put in new coffee or just run water through the grounds from seven days ago. Wood took his coffee down to his office, where he sat all day devising strategies to compensate for the lost revenue caused by the storm and Debbie's departure, leaving Tony in the showroom to quietly contemplate the components she had fixed. He thought of her capable hands and the commission he would make selling those items, which he didn't feel was right. Debbie had shown them a new way for Stereoblast, a brighter way, and now they were left with only her shadow.

When Agathe approached Tony from the backroom, she could feel it: the pull of sadness. She went directly to one of the stereos and turned it on. Cheap Trick wanted her to want them. Tony nodded yes to Cheap Trick.

The two of them listened to the radio all day, playing songs that reminded them of Debbie, and not a single customer came through the doors. At five o'clock, Tony took the untouched till down to Wood, who told him to go on ahead, he had some things to finish downstairs. Tony tried to smile as he passed Agathe.

"Tomorrow'll be better," he said.

"Ouah, ben sûr," she said.

Wood chose to stay late. Agathe had planned to skip the vacuuming, but with him sitting downstairs she would have to. Stupid Wood. She cranked the volume on the radio. It played what sounded like a medley of different guitar parts all belonging to different songs, and she knew right away it was Kansas and their wayward son. Agathe only knew the chorus, but she shouted along as she jerked the vacuum hose carelessly across the floor, deaf to the sensor on the sliding door that she hadn't bothered to lock—and to the sound of JC and Réjean locking it behind them from the inside.

As a man with agricultural interests, the Colonel kept meticulously abreast of weather trends, and consulted the *Farmer's Almanac* every season to find out what preparations to make for his grapes. He had known about the storm months in advance and had made arrangements for the crops, as well as all temperature-sensitive areas of the compound that accommodated the fragile storage and aging needs of cheeses and wines. In the fall, he had assigned the task to JC of buying up every reasonably priced space heater he could find. Four of the heaters were set up in the Pinot Noir quadrant of the greenhouse, an extremely delicate grape, and the one upon which the Colonel had staked his reputation. He had buyers lining up seasons in advance for crates of his Pinot Noir.

JC had bought those four heaters at Stereoblast. Tony had started the sale, suggesting the two working heaters in the showroom. When Wood, eavesdropping nearby, overheard the details, he thought of the Possibility Pile, and stepped in. The heaters Wood had been hoarding in the Possibility Pile made noise when you turned them on, but produced no heat. Wood sold them to JC nonetheless, and they had been responsible for the loss of an entire crop of grapes.

JC waved to Réjean, poked a finger into his own chest, then pointed it down the stairs, making a pair of walking legs with his index and middle fingers. He pointed at Réjean, then at the floor. Réjean pointed wide-eyed at Agathe, whose back remained to them, and JC replied by making a zipping motion against his lips, then disappeared along the wall and out of sight down the stairs.

Agathe vacuumed vigorously. "Carray hon," she yelled.

Réjean assumed a position behind her like a goalie, trying to skirt her line of vision, but there was no rhyme or reason to her aim of the duct-taped hose. She faked him out a few times as he tried his best to remain out of sight.

Réjean hadn't laid a hand on anyone since the cheese idiot's death. At night, he dreamed he was a monster, stomping on houses, destroying towns for no reason. In these dreams, he saw screaming peasants in typical scenes of storybook destruction, but also the greater human detail of the damage he had wrought: the orphans, widows, terror, grief, and inconvenience of disaster. He would wake up wanting to flee from himself. His guilt had begun affecting his dealings with the Colonel and the other men. No one could get near him. And now, the possibility of hurting the woman in the electronics store was making him sweaty and feverish.

Through the noise of vacuum and radio, Agathe's intuition sent her a signal. She stiffened, ears cocked, and Réjean braced himself against the wall. He had been detected. He dove to the right as she spun around to her left. She spun to her right and he leaped to her left. He could feel her fear and knew she was going to scream, and so with no alternative, he threw an arm around her middle and another around her face, covering her mouth. She writhed wildly, forcing him to tighten his grip, filling him with dread.

Agathe could feel the mossy softness of his beard tickling the top of her head. With her nose free for breathing, she inhaled deeply and her senses sounded the alarm. From the hand over her mouth came a scent that created a stampede in her guts and pierced her heart. She began to hyperventilate and fought with everything she had, all elbows, grunting and raging beneath the giant hand, trying to get a look. It was him. It was *him*.

Réjean was queasy with the violence of just holding her, but now that she was struggling and he had to squeeze the globe of her upper half close enough to smell her Craven As, he realized with horror what was happening to him. He was getting an erection. Not just any erection, but an unruly one, jutting and huge, demanding to be known. He squirmed sideways to keep it from poking into her. She continued to writhe with every ounce of her strength, arms and legs flailing, forcing him to hold her tighter, picking her up just off the floor so that her feet dangled. He breathed through his mouth to keep from being sick. There was more fight in her than he could ever have guessed. She started to kick and bite, refusing defeat, and Réjean, unable to keep up with the sheer force of her resistance, shook her free onto the floor.

She gaped up at him with the whites of her eyes showing. It was him. Under the inexplicable beard, his perfect face, his eyes, the cheeks she had kissed millions of times, and the hair that curled around the backs of his ears. It was him. She beamed back at him, but nothing in his face, in his big, soft brows, in his deep, black eyes, told her he knew her. Instead, they told her of apprehension. When he turned his back on her to adjust his pants, she threw herself on him.

"Réjean, Réjean," she cried, kissing him and pulling him closer.

He grabbed her wrists, the force of his restraint making him queasier, and held her up in front of him as she panted and made strange, dovelike noises. His eyes explored her face. He didn't know her.

"Réjean," she said again, losing strength. "Réjean, Réjean, Réjean."

The relief of touching him, looking at him, completely alive before her, made her want to sob hot, heavy tears, to melt into him and absorb his strength the way she had the first time she lay her hands on him. Instead, she collapsed into his chest, wheezing, sockets dry.

Réjean was convinced to go home with Agathe mostly through his shame at having manhandled her in the store and his inability to follow her frenzied explanation of their life together. All the way home, Agathe fought the urge to pull the Silverado over to the side of the road and dive on top of him. His distracted stare held her at bay. Since the Silverado hadn't sparked anything for Réjean, Agathe turned on the French folk station at a nearly audible volume, but he didn't notice. Testing him, she tuned the radio to her usual station, and the song about girls with fat bottoms was playing. So she turned it up just a little, and a sourness spread across Réjean's face. He looked at her quizzically as she nodded her head to the rhythm.

"Freddie Mercury, ça," she said.

He turned toward the window and rested his head against the frame.

When they pulled into the driveway and their home appeared in the clearing, she checked him again. As he took in the little cottage through the window, a look of disbelief crossed his face, followed by a frown.

Martin was in the kitchen, setting the table for dinner. "Fourchette, couteau, fourchette," he mused as he flanked the dinner plates. When Réjean ducked his head through the front door, Martin froze, the final couteau clutched in his petrified fist. Seeing Réjean alive, his first impulse was to scream or cry, but as the moment stretched on, he caught the hint of difference in Réjean. He wasn't looking at Martin at all, but glancing disappointedly around the kitchen. Only when Agathe introduced them did he realize that not only did Réjean not know him, he was unfamiliar with the sound of his own name.

Agathe led Réjean from room to room, hoping one of them would set something off in his memory, as Martin, still holding a butter knife in the kitchen, felt a trickle of sweat roll down his side. Truth had become mercurial with Martin as its custodian, and Réjean's memory threatened to connect the dots of reality. So many times while he and Agathe had sat playing cards he thought of telling her the truth. If he was going to say something, now was the time. Or was it? He vowed to give it some more thought and come up with a better moment. But he would tell them. It was the right thing to do. For now, he watched as Agathe clicked the lights on and off in each room, the big plaid shirt growing damp around him.

Over the next week, Réjean stayed on for the possibility of something triggering his memory. He and Martin spent the days playing gin rummy while Agathe was at work, Réjean trying to picture what the Colonel and the guys might be up to, Martin breathlessly anticipating a glimpse of recollection in Réjean's face. Martin perspired like he hadn't since Réjean's disappearance, unable to say the thing he needed to, letting moment after moment pass until it was too late. And yet, with each day that Réjean's memory remained truant, Martin's sense of security within the household solidified.

While she enjoyed the company and the help around the house, Agathe was losing her patience with Réjean's mind. Her hope for its return faded a little each time he stroked his beard. He didn't seem to want to remember. They performed the outward rituals of married people, without the private advantages that set them apart from any other two humans who shared meals and a home. By Réjean's design, they didn't touch at all. He had a way of making sure there was something physical separating them at all times; he would make sure that a chair, or Martin, was between them. Being in bed was the toughest part. Pyjama-clad, with nothing in the way, they lay side by side, Réjean squeezing his eyes shut the moment he was under the covers, Agathe waiting for him to turn over and let her know it was okay to go ahead, even if he didn't remember her. But he just lay there, playing possum. The first few nights, she felt she might explode, being so close to his body, so close to the mouth she couldn't kiss, struggling with his heat and smell. But after a week had passed, she found she was again able to sleep through the night. She never stopped hoping to feel the pressure of his hand on her body, but as they lay there, she found it increasingly easy to just shrug it off and turn over.

As she pulled into the drive for another Friday night with her new family, she saw the brown envelope from Sondage on the front step. Holding the envelope fondly, she glanced up to see Martin and Réjean looking down at their cards in their usual spots at the kitchen table and pursed her lips.

They ate a chicken fricot in silence, and Agathe checked the clock periodically, trying to imagine what Debbie might be doing, where, and with whom. Suddenly, she said, "Voulez-vous faire quelque chose de fun asoir?"

After dinner, the three of them climbed into the Silverado and headed for the Convenience Place liquor store.

Back at home, Agathe twisted off the top of a beer, working on the beginnings of a callus like the one Debbie had between her thumb and forefinger. Martin poured himself a rum, offered one to Réjean, and tried to hide his disappointment when Réjean declined, dreamily opening a bottle of Bordeaux. Friday nights, at Colonel Weed's, JC would make a roast and they would drink gallons of wine as the Colonel and his men shared work stories. Réjean never tired of those stories and wondered if maybe, at that moment, they might be telling stories about him.

They sat awkwardly for a minute before Martin lifted his rum. Agathe and Réjean followed, Réjean said, "Beunh," and they drank.

Booze made cards more fun. It also made it possible, after Agathe had laid down her fifth gin rummy, for Réjean to be able to carelessly reach out and smack her on the arm. They drank and played, and the house filled with smoke and noise. The looser they got, the more Agathe started to recognize in Réjean the man she once knew and the more urgently she wanted to get him to the bedroom. Before long, Martin collapsed sitting up in his chair, his head flopped forward. Agathe reached out and grabbed the front of Réjean's shirt, pushed him all the way down the hall, and opened the door with his back. When she had directed him to the bed, she threw him down and climbed on top of him, undoing his top shirt button with glee. Réjean, unprepared, only recognized what was happening once he was on the bed and felt the same horrified arousal he had at Stereoblast. His defences kicked in and, without thinking, he flung her off him, into the air, where she seemed to float for a moment before landing on the floor with a muffled thud.

He held his breath, frozen.

The throbbing mass inside her was now working its way to her extremities. This feeling was new, different from the propulsion of sadness or longing, of irritation, boredom, or love. This one made the tips of her fingers and toes burn. She clamped her mouth shut as an unexpected catalogue of words queued up for escape. She knew that, for all the anguish he caused her, he wasn't really to blame. He simply didn't know what they'd lost.

But the force would not be contained for long. She flipped over, found her feet, and dusted herself off before retreating briskly to the kitchen. She strained with every muscle to hold in the storm, but when she saw Martin at the kitchen table, still passed out, she broke for just a second to lift his hat and ruffle the soft, flattened hair underneath. He moaned and, without opening his eyes, said, "I was there. With him."

She stopped, her hand dangling over his head.

"I was there. Wi' Réjean. Wen he disappeard," he mused into his lap. "He din' disappear...he was hit. B' truck. Took him away. I was there. Withim. I mento tell you, I men to tell...you. He was gon. But now he's here, eh. Amazing...I ate sanwich..."

The words threaded through her ears like a marquee ribbon. All this time, he had known. He had known. All this time. She grabbed him by the shoulders and shook him until his head snapped back. His eyes flashed with lucidity and he heard the echo of the words that had just left his mouth.

"You knew?" she said, trembling.

"Oh God," he said.

Agathe stood a moment longer, trying to take in the man she had fed and nursed like a baby bird. And when she looked at him, and thought of a baby bird, she thought of tiny bones and eggs, and she imagined how a knuckle might shatter an eye socket, the crackling sound it might make, like breaking a little blue shell.

She pushed Martin back, then jerked her hands away from him, and grabbed her coat. As she thrust her arm into the second sleeve, she turned back to him slowly, darkness filling her mind.

"You...ate...his...lunch..." She hissed, as Martin gazed back in terror.

"Oh," he said. "God."

She had never felt the urge to hurt something so badly, nor felt so certain she could. As she backed away from Martin, Réjean appeared out of the darkness of the hallway, wearing his coat.

"Agathe," he said softly.

His voice was so intimate that she suddenly turned with every expectation of Réjean, the real one, standing there. But it was only that bearded stranger. She glared back at him, daring him to speak, but he cast his gaze downward and uttered the only thing he could find the voice to express. "Beunh..."

Agathe tore her keys from the wall, pulling the nail free, and Réjean and Martin winced as it tinkled onto the floor.

Inside the Silverado, she revved the engine, idling in front of the kitchen window long enough to watch Martin throw his sobbing face down on his arms and Réjean place a reassuring palm on his shoulder—a gesture of compassion she seethed to think he would never have offered her.

Flooring the accelerator, her gaze fixed on a pinpoint of road, she pitched through the night. Thoughts of Martin and Réjean, the past, the future, Stereoblast, bombarded her from all sides. As each one threatened to touch down, she sped up, fending them off with unharnessed momentum. Ardently, fixedly, she drove.

As her thoughts intensified their attack, she crouched down so that her chin was nearly touching the wheel and concentrated on the clear path ahead until the space between her eyebrows throbbed. She became vaguely aware of a coldness in her eyes from not blinking.

Trooper asked her why, if she didn't like what she saw, she didn't change it.

As her focus narrowed, her thoughts were forced outward and began spinning in a sort of centrifuge in her mind, pulling gravitationally to the edges of her consciousness. With one ear cocked for sirens, she glanced into the eternity of woodland whipping past. The wildness would be thrashing uncontrolled in there right now, braying and roaring—the very lawlessness taking her over—and she wanted to get closer, to plunge into its depths. She took the first turn off the main road and peeled down a snow-covered gravel lane, rolling to a stop at the verge of a frozen lake.

Before her spread a clean, white spill of undisturbed snow girded by a belt of forest. As she inhaled deeply in the stillness, her senses newly alert, a thought whiffed down at her from the spinning mass. It was a flash of Réjean, opening his arms to hold her. She sucked in her breath but did not turn away. With all its torment, she looked right at it, letting it pummel her, forcing on her the reality that it would only ever be the past. That new things needed to happen now, because it was urgent. The pain was unlike anything she had ever felt, but she absorbed the shock. Hydraulically.

The very idea, now that she'd found him, of releasing Réjean back into the ether was unfathomable. But the sensation of waking up every day and wanting him, like a pheasant under glass, so close but impossible to touch, was a thousand times worse than lying amid his shirts, wondering what had become of him. Being the object of his discomfort hurt infinitely more than imagining him stroking another woman's hair and laughing about how Agathe would never find him. She had seen and felt enough of his trepidation to know that it defined him now, just as his love for her once had. Just as the empty expectation of his return had defined her.

Trooper told her to see how it felt to raise a little hell of her own.

She grabbed the gearshift, stomped down on the accelerator, and launched out onto the white. She shifted up and cut a track straight across the ice. Just as she was about to hit the shore, she seized the emergency brake and sent the Silverado spinning out in loops.

As she tore across her own wheel skids, grinding the half shafts, and as her thoughts spun in her mind, stuck to the sides, another process was taking place in the core of the eddy. It was hallucinogenic at first, uncontrollable, like malaria or anesthetic, then slowly crystallized, becoming tangible. Literal. She was losing mass and tension. Her top half was decompressing, her spine straightening, her eyes retracting into their sockets.

She hooted, her breath barking out hard as the truck slid sideways and she reached hand-over-hand to bring it under control. She threw back her head and shrieked, put it into gear and burned toward the opposite shore. Again, she grabbed the brake and spun out, then back into gear, driving one big circle all the way around the shore, howling out the window.

She finally came to rest in the middle of the river, the once-pristine snow ravaged by her tire tracks, and she panted, admiring her work, illuminated by the headlights.

With a final salute to the trees, she brought the Silverado back up onto land and through the wooded path to the road. As she waited with the turn signal blinking, a transport truck passed her by, and she pictured herself at the wheel with the radio blasting, soaring past the other cars. She made a note of the number on the door. 1-800-WED-RIVE.

The sky ahead sparkled with the glow of late-night commerce. This world still amazed her. People who didn't watch TV or play cards at the kitchen table, who went out after dinner—who ate dinner outside their own homes. It was all so new, filled with the promise that things could be different. Here, you could sing to yourself.

The noise pulsing from the Whisky Mak pulled her like a magnet past the sedans and hatchbacks and trucks to the big red doors, where she inhaled deeply before throwing them open.

She ordered an Alpine and glanced at the two solitary women in their same spots across the bar. When her beer arrived, she lifted it judiciously in their direction. They lifted their drinks in return.

Scanning the ocean of heads, she found him almost instantly, perhaps because of his attire, because he was the only person seated at a table alone, or because to Agathe he shone like the high beams.

Bruce started singing a song about madmen and bummers and drummers and a hundred other things.

The mass of noise and bodies blurred into uniform darkness around the army man's glow. Agathe picked up her beer and pushed off the bar rail with her toe, headed for the light.

ACKNOWLEDGEMENTS

Thanks to Tor Brodkorb, Kevin Cogliano, Anne Drew, Maria Eleftheriou, Sarah Heinonen, Scott Hildebrandt, Laura Martin, Marko Sijan, and Jacques Viau for your sharp eyes and helpful comments, to Leigh Nash for believing in this book and helping me chisel it down to a fighting machine, to Stuart Ross for things too numerous to count, but namely for teaching me to write and for championing this book like a champion, and to my only, only Lori Delorme, for bottomless support, tireless readings, and for being my best friend.

INVISIBLE PUBLISHING is a not-for-profit publishing company that produces contemporary works of fiction, creative non-fiction, and poetry. We're small in scale, but we take our work, and our mission, seriously: We publish material that's engaging, literary, current, and uniquely Canadian.

We are committed to publishing diverse voices and experiences. In acknowledging historical and systemic barriers, and the limits of our existing catalogue, we strongly encourage writers of colour to submit their work.

Invisible Publishing continues to produce high-quality literary works, and we're also home to the Bibliophonic series, Snare, and Throwback imprints.

If you'd like to know more please get in touch:
info@invisiblepublishing.com

Invisible Publishing
Halifax & Picton